Praise for *Codenan*

D0498831

'Leo Kanaris takes us to post-crash Athens as austerity ~~~
and political corruption spirals... *Codename Xenophon* is
compelling and evocative (the sparkling sea and sun)...
Kanaris has written a little gem, perfect for the beach.'

Scarlet MccGuire in *Tribune*

'Blessed with all the virtues of a traditional murder mystery,
this debut novel has a sharp political edge. Three years in
Athens left Leo Kanaris with a loathing for the self-serving
parasites and bureaucrats who "had paralysed the country for
decades". In *Codename Xenophon*, this insider's view of a
paralytic society is seen through the eyes of George Zafiris,
a private investigator who does his best to tread the straight
and narrow, while those around him are too greedy or plain
scared to take responsibility. It is the apparently motiveless
killing of an elderly academic that embroils Zafiris in
political machinations at the highest level. But, as his dogged
perseverance begins to pay off, he comes to realise that even
the best intentions can have tragic consequences. With vivid
characterisation and a plot that thickens without obscuring the
essential threads, Kanaris emerges as a sharp new talent in
crime writing.'
Barry Turner in *The Daily Mail*

'The narrative flits from a frenzied Athens to the idyllic islands
as politicians, Russian crooks, corrupt (and/or incompetent)
policemen thicken the plot, the world-weary Zafiris nimbly
negotiating a Byzantine culture in which morality, truth and
justice are malleable concepts. The first in a proposed quartet
to feature George Zafiris, *Codename Xenophon* is a bleak
but blackly comic tale that does full justice to its laconic,
Chandleresque heritage.' Declan Burke in *The Irish Times*

Praise for *Blood & Gold*:

'Those of us who are both Graecophiles and lovers of good thrillers have been a little short of material since Paul Johnston called time on his Anglo-Greek private eye Alex Mavros and the Inspector Haritos policiers of Petros Markaris ceased to enjoy English translations. Now, however, Anglo-Greek Leo Kanaris who writes in English but lives in Greece, has filled the void. Cops rather than private eyes are the norm these days, at least in Europe, but Kanaris has reverted to the Chandleresque tradition. George Zafiris is no ex-cop or disgraced DA, though – he's a former economist at Greece's Central Bank! It's an unlikely change of profession, but one that allows Kanaris to create a crime-busting hero without the gung-ho characteristics of some of his literary counterparts... This series is an intelligent, engrossing treat.'

Mike Parker in *Tribune*

'*Blood and Gold*, and an earlier thriller by Leo Kanaris, *Codename Xenophon*, are perfect examples of how well-crafted detective fiction from another country opens windows on to a brave new world, and shows that there are more similarities than differences between us all as we get on with the business of living in failing Western societies. As the post-war liberal bandwagon begins to roll backwards, overtaken by the populist demagogue's juggernaut of lies, we need more cracking good crime stories like this one, to entertain, illuminate, and inform.' Georgia de Chamberet in *Book Blast*

'Kanaris depicts a troubled Greece with compassion and precisely observed social commentary.' *Publishers Weekly*

Leo Kanaris

DANGEROUS DAYS

Dedalus

Supported using public funding by
ARTS COUNCIL
ENGLAND

Published in the UK by Dedalus Limited
24-26, St Judith's Lane, Sawtry, Cambs, PE28 5XE
email: info@dedalusbooks.com
www.dedalusbooks.com

ISBN printed book 978 1 910213 71 1
ISBN ebook 978 1 912868 17 9

Dedalus is distributed in the USA & Canada by SCB Distributors
15608 South New Century Drive, Gardena, CA 90248
email: info@scbdistributors.com   web: www.scbdistributors.com

Dedalus is distributed in Australia by Peribo Pty Ltd
58, Beaumont Road, Mount Kuring-gai, N.S.W. 2080
email: info@peribo.com.au

First published by Dedalus in 2019

Printed and bound in Great Britain by Clays Elcograf S.p.A
Typeset by Marie Lane

A C.I.P. listing for this book is available on request.

The Author

Leo Kanaris was a teacher for many years. He now writes full time and lives in southern Greece.

He is the author of three novels featuring the private investigator George Zafiris: *Codename Xenophon*, *Blood & Gold* and *Dangerous Days*.

He is currently working on his fourth George Zafiris novel.

You enter Greece as one might enter a dark crystal; the form of things becomes irregular, refracted… Wherever you look the trembling curtain of the atmosphere deceives.
Lawrence Durrell, *Prospero's Cell*

Με πλήγωσες και δεν ξεχνώ.
You wounded me and I don't forget.
Marika Ninou & Vassilis Tsitsanis, 'Γεννήθηκα να πονώ'
('I was born to suffer')

And it seems like it goes on like this for ever.
James Taylor, 'Carolina In My Mind'

Characters
(in order of appearance)

George Zafiris – private investigator
Zoe Zafiris – wife of George
Maria Katramis – Zoe's cousin, a tax official
Stelios Katramis – Maria's husband; a building contractor
Pandelís Katramis – son of Stelios and Maria
Olli Papaspirou – girlfriend of Pandelís Katramis, a student
Wasim Khan – Pakistani farm worker
Nick Zafiris – son of George and Zoe Zafiris
Colonel Sotiriou – Head of the Violent Crimes Department, Athens Police
Haris Pezas – owner of an electrical shop, assistant of George Zafiris
Yiannis Koroneos – George Zafiris' lawyer
Dimitri – proprietor of the Café Agamemnon in Aristotle Street
Flamur Zamir – retired circus acrobat and transport entrepreneur
Fisnik Zamir – Flamur's twin brother
Leonidas Papaspirou – a businessman, father of Olli
Antigone Papaspirou – mother of Olli
Manolis – farm supervisor

Pavlos Lazaridis – eminent lawyer

Christos Mazis – teacher at Athens College

Sonia Venieri – tax auditor

Mihali – head of security at the Yerakas estate

Sebastian Yerakas – farm owner from Marathon

Simeon Yerakas – Sebastian's father, a wealthy property developer

Dr Galini – a doctor, related to Sonia Venieri

Byron Kakridis – Minister of Development

Jerry Kasimatis – a Greek-American in the construction business

Margaret – a Scottish neighbour of Haris Pezas

Dino – Colonel Sotiriou's driver

1

Sunday lunch, January 2018. A seaside tavern near Marathon. Cold sunshine, a brisk wind whipping the tops off the short, choppy waves. The light glitters in salty splinters through roll-down polythene walls. Families sit at long tables, shoulders hunched, forks stabbing at fried fish, voices clashing in the greasy air. Hungry cats crouch around the tables. They pounce on every scrap, hissing and fighting off rivals with slashing claws.

George Zafiris sits with his wife Zoe and a group of relatives: Zoe's cousin Maria, her husband Stelios, their son Pandelís and his girlfriend Olli. Stelios and Maria have a weekend house nearby, but they always eat out on Sundays. Zoe is talking to Maria, a tax inspector who does a good line in loud and indignant comment on the failings of the Greek State. George is stuck in a conversation with Stelios about the building trade. Stelios knows all about this, it's his business, but he fails to open up on the subject. Or on any subject. Pale, dull-eyed, paunchy and unfit, dressed with expensive bad taste, he wears a jaded, bitter expression, as if he has seen and suffered every rip-off, lie, con-trick and fraud in the world. He treats all communication, even with George, as a disguised attempt to cheat him out of money. He has plenty of it, even in these impossible times; no one knows why or how, but it could be something to do with his wife's job, which is one of the most lucrative in the entire mechanism of the state.

George can sense Stelios sniffing for hidden motives in every word he says. As George is a detective, he listens with equal suspicion to everything Stelios says, and their lunchtime dialogue is a strange, distorting experience, like walking in a hall of mirrors.

Pandelís is a good-looking young man with a ready smile and flashing, lecherous eyes. Employed as an intern at an investment bank in London, he has picked up the self-confident air of his Anglo-Saxon colleagues. He is being groomed to take over the family business, and takes prosperity, good luck and pretty girls for granted. Olli, a florid, black-eyed beauty, is studying marketing at Patras University. She keeps a close grip on her fiancé's attention. There is something unusual about her, an intensity, a thoughtfulness, a hint of pain. She and Pandelís talk in low voices about subjects of their own, aloof from the lumbering predictabilities of the older generation.

The purpose of the lunch, the reason why George has to sit it out politely, is to talk Stelios into offering a job to their son Nick. This is Zoe's idea, fast becoming an obsession. George goes along with it for the sake of a quiet life. Like half the young population of Greece, Nick faces unemployment as soon as he completes his studies. Zoe has been telling everyone what a brilliant student he is, what a noble character, how ambitious, loyal and diligent, what an asset he would be to any company. Stelios and Maria are aware of the game being played. They have responded with a set of well-oiled platitudes about the harsh economic climate and the need for young people to turn their hands to anything, unpaid if necessary. 'Look at Pandelís,' says Maria. 'His job in London costs us money. Internships are standard in England and America. Why not here too? Do we want to be modern or not?'

George keeps quiet, his attention drifting to the olive trees outside, their leaves changing colour from silver to green and back again in the vagaries of the wind.

He loves his son and wants him to get a good job, but the fact is, he could do with some work himself.

Times are hard in Greece. Eight years of financial crisis, and still no end in sight. A pitiless austerity programme imposed by the European Union and the International Monetary Fund has been so incompetently administered that it has wrecked the productive sectors of the economy while fattening the state bureaucracy. Every year that passes feels like a step back into a grim and hopeless past. The atmosphere is bleak. Detective work, like many traditional professions, is virtually dead. Even that old investigator's standby, the extra-marital affair, has gone into hibernation. What happened to all that uncontrolled Greek libido? Is that too in short supply – like cash?

A movement catches George's eye. Distorted by the ripples in the plastic walls, a figure is tottering unsteadily towards the taverna from the road. Weaving, lurching, grasping at the empty air.

For a few moments George watches him, not quite believing what he is seeing. Then he makes hurriedly for the door.

Out in the car park the man twists like a flame and falls. His head thuds into the ground. He lies face down, his black hair wild and matted with blood, his clothes dusty and torn.

He looks like a piece of rubbish. George picks up the man's hand to feel for a pulse. As he counts the feeble heartbeats he notices the dark colour of the skin.

Stelios has followed him out.

'What's going on?'

'Can you call an ambulance?' says George.

'Is he alive?'

'Just about.'

Stelios dips a hand into his trouser pocket, pulls out a phone and contemplates it as if he has forgotten what it does.

'What's the problem?' asks George impatiently.

'Nothing. I just remembered something else.'

Slowly, Stelios dials the emergency number. In his heavy voice he says, 'I am calling you from Marathon, outside the *Thalassaki* fish taverna. We have an unknown man, a Pakistani or Indian, unconscious, bleeding. He may have been in a fight. We need an ambulance.' He gives the address, then flares with sudden indignation: 'No! Why the hell should you have my name? Just get over here!' and hangs up.

Together, carefully, they turn the man over and raise his head. The face is bruised and swollen, a gash over the right eye smeared with blood and dust. Pressing a bottle of water to the man's lips, George gets no response. He tilts the bottle, letting the water pour over the man's chin. He tips the bottle over the forehead, bathing the whole face. The tongue appears, hesitant, between cracked lips.

The eyes flicker open, bewildered and afraid.

George tells him not to worry. 'The ambulance will be here soon,' he says. 'It will take you to the hospital.'

'No!' The man protests with sudden vigour. 'No hospital!'

'You need a doctor.'

'No!'

'He's an illegal,' says Stelios with disgust.

'Obviously,' says George.

The man coughs weakly, a barely visible shudder in his chest.

'Jesus,' says Stelios, 'he's in a bad way.'

George takes out his phone and searches for Colonel Sotiriou, Head of the Violent Crimes Unit. He dials the number. The response is hostile, even worse than usual.

'Zafiris? Why the hell are you calling me on a Sunday?'

'Forgive me Colonel, this is urgent.'

'What's got into you?'

'I need a favour, Colonel.'

'When do you not?'

'I've got a Pakistani migrant worker out here in Marathon. He's been done over, badly injured. He's terrified of going to hospital. Can you cover him?'

'What do you mean, cover him?'

'Make sure they don't give him trouble with his papers?'

'Why?'

'Looks like a violent crime to me, possibly racist.'

'Call the duty officer.'

'I need your personal help.'

'No you don't.'

'I don't ask lightly, Colonel.'

'Will you leave me alone for the rest of my life?'

'Gladly.'

'Right. Tell me the name of the hospital and the individual concerned.'

'When I know I'll tell you.'

The Colonel hung up, leaving a heavy silence.

As the ambulance appeared, the Pakistani made an attempt to stand up. His muscles failed him.

'Take it easy,' said George. 'You won't be deported. I've spoken to the police.'

'No police!' cried the man.

'No police,' said George. 'Only a doctor. Tell me your name.'

'No name!'

'I must have your name or I cannot help you.'

Very reluctantly and weakly the man pronounced two syllables: 'Wa-sim.'

'Family name?'

'Khan.'

'Where do you live?'

Wasim pointed vaguely towards a clump of scrubby bushes.

'How far?'

He gave no reply. The paramedics were now standing over him, eager to get on. After a brief examination they lifted him onto a stretcher.

'Where will you take him?' asked George.

'KAT.'

'So far?'

'It's the nearest public hospital.'

George walked with them to the ambulance. Wasim stared blankly at him. As the paramedics strapped him down, his eyes flashed with a fearful appeal. George gave an encouraging wave as the doors closed.

Stelios was waiting for him in the car park. He seemed troubled.

'Why are you bothered about that guy? Do you know him?'

'No.'

'So why get involved?'

'You know the answer.'

'I do not know the answer! This is why I'm asking.'

'In other circumstances that could have been you or me. Imagine if you were in his country and someone mugged you. Would you want to be left to die in a car park?'

'I don't plan to go to Pakistan.'

'That's irrelevant. It could just as well happen here. Or in New York.'

'I have no wish to visit his godforsaken land. Why the hell should he come to mine?'

'So that you can pay 50 cents for a kilo of tomatoes instead of 85.'

'Makes no difference to me.'

'Really? You're very lucky then.'

'My wife does the shopping.'

'Oh great. That absolves you, I suppose!'

'I have no interest in these people. They mean nothing to me. They're just trouble.'

'Remember the parable of the Good Samaritan?'

'Don't start preaching at me, George. I have enough problems of my own without taking on all your shit.'

'If you call compassion "shit" I feel sorry for you.'

'Leave it, George. Go and break someone else's balls.'

Back at the table, Stelios sat down grumpily and began forking bundles of cold chips into his mouth. George was too upset to eat any more. He pushed his plate away.

'What happened?' asked Zoe, sensing the tension between them, trying to brighten things up.

'Ask the Good Samaritan,' said Stelios.

'We helped a Pakistani,' said George. 'A man who had been beaten up.'

'So?'

'Stelios thought it was a mistake.'

'Oh? Why?'

There was an awkward silence.

'Stelios can't stand Pakistanis,' said Maria. 'Or Bangladeshis.'

'It's not that…' he objected feebly.

'Or Indians,' Maria continued. 'Or Africans. Any of the really foreign-looking types. We don't mind Filippinos, because they're polite, they work hard, but the others – *Apapá! Makriá!*' She fluttered her hands disgustedly.

'It's not a question of liking or disliking,' said George. 'The man was injured. And Stelios was kind enough to telephone the ambulance.'

'Well, that's perfect then! You've done a good turn. Now you can eat your lunch and forget about it.'

George could eat no more, but he did his best to forget – with scant success. He listened wearily to the conversation. Stelios livened up somewhat and began complaining about the government. 'I'm angry,' he said. 'Very angry! Mr Tsipras claimed to offer a way out of austerity. He was elected on that promise, but all he does is strangle business. Taxes, more taxes and regulations. Why? Because let's face it, he's a communist. A typical communist. Destroying the economy, destroying lives, all in the name of the impossible ideal of equality.'

'The Europeans are to blame too,' said Pandelís. 'Specially the Germans. They tricked us into this austerity with their easy loans, their single currency, and now they tie our hands! We are their slaves. It's the old German dream, achieved without military conquest.'

'Are the Germans dreaming or are we?' said Zoe. 'I feel we've been sleepwalking for the past ten years. Through the dark, with our eyes closed. Towards a terrible place. A deep hole. A chasm. Towards a…'

'Grexit perhaps?' offered Pandelís.

'Maybe!'

'Would that really be so bad?'

'It would be a total bloody disaster,' said Stelios.

'Why, father?'

'It's one of the most idiotic suggestions anybody has made.'

'Why do you say that? At least we'd get away from the euro and the tentacles of Brussels.'

'I'm not going to talk about it now. It's upsetting me.'

'Come on, tell me! Or I'll think you're avoiding the question.'

'Do you know how much we import into this country, my boy?' He held up his hand and counted on his fingers. 'Petrol, fuel oil, natural gas, food, clothes, plastics, medicines, cars, tractors, electrical goods, machinery… Billions and billions' worth every year! If we leave the euro, go back to the drachma, we'll *immediately* devalue. Everything will double in price overnight. You want that? You think the Greek people want that? Maybe that idiot Tsipras wants it because the whole economy would collapse!'

'At least we would be able to control our monetary policy.'

'Control! From a position of total weakness? I don't think so!'

'No way forward and no way back,' said Zoe.

'This is getting depressing.' said Maria. 'Let's order coffee. Who wants an espresso?'

With the meal dragging turgidly to its end, and the subject of Nick still unmentioned, George made a supreme effort. What were the chances, he asked, that Stelios might find their son a job?

Stelios was matter-of-fact. 'Tell him to send me his CV. I don't have any openings right now but you never know.'

'We rely on you,' said Zoe.

'Better not,' said Stelios.

George thanked him and called for the bill, which he insisted on paying.

2

As soon as George swung his Alfa Romeo out of the car park, Zoe opened up. 'What the hell were you playing at? You spent the whole lunch scowling at everybody as if you thought they were stupid, then you ran off to deal with some random Pakistani. After that you insulted Stelios. Aren't you prepared to do anything for your son's future?'

'I asked the question, didn't I?'

'Oh yes. You asked the question, like you'd swing an axe. A peasant would have made a better job of it.'

'No doubt.'

'What have you got against Stelios?'

'He's a bore.'

'A bore who happens to be rich!'

'I don't think he's the right man to approach.'

'Who is the right man? Your Pakistani?'

'Don't be stupid. First we need to talk to Nick, see what he wants to do.'

'*Wants?*' Zoe glared at him in disbelief. 'Who gets what he *wants* these days? He'll be lucky to get a job at all.'

'He's an engineer, Zoe. Engineers are always in demand.'

'And you were once an economist. Look where that got you.'

'We're talking about Nick.'

'I'm talking about money, George!'

'Let's stay with Nick for now, shall we?'

'Oh yes, why not? Nice safe subject!'

'You brought it up. This whole shitty day was your idea.'

'It wasn't shitty until you made it shitty.'

'No, I would definitely say it had "shitty" written all over it from the start.'

Zoe gave him a disgusted look.

'The fact is,' she said, 'Nick needs to come home and get a job. End of story. He's been in England long enough.'

'That's up to him.'

'It is not up to him! Young people don't know what they're doing. They need guidance. He should come back here, find a nice girl from a good family, build his career…'

'What career? The economy's bust.'

'There are always jobs for those who are prepared to work.'

'With 50% unemployment? I don't think so.'

'You've always got some smart-ass answer.'

'It's not a smart-ass answer, it's the truth.'

'I'm not talking about statistics,' said Zoe. 'I'm talking about opportunities. There are some lovely girls around. Look at Olli. She's gorgeous, her parents are wealthy, they're first class people… I can think of at least three ship-owners' daughters who are on the look-out for husbands now. Nick's missing out.'

'Those girls won't marry a man without a job.'

'Let them fall in love first. If he goes for the right girl, her father will give him a job.'

'How cynical you are.'

'I look at it practically.'

'You look at the money and ignore everything else.'

'Do you blame me?'

'How many friends do we have, Zoe, who married for money and now regret it?'

'Not as many as those who regret *not* marrying for money! Which includes me, by the way.'

'Thanks,' said George, wounded by the remark.

'And we *are* going to talk about money now,' Zoe went on, 'because I'm worried. Worried and totally fed up. When we got married you had a steady job at the bank. You seemed happy. You never told me that you planned to chuck it all in to become a private detective. With no regular income, no pension, and a bloody good chance of getting killed! Like your poor friend Hector.'

'I didn't *plan* to leave the bank.'

'Oh? It was an impulse was it? That's even worse!'

'It was neither a plan nor an impulse'

'So what was it?'

'It was a feeling.'

'A feeling! Ha!'

'A feeling that grew inside me, over several years, until it became a conviction.'

'So now it's a conviction?'

'I knew I had to stop working at the bank.'

'You didn't *have* to stop. Did they force you to go?'

'No.'

'So why?'

'I don't like explaining it when you're in such a vile mood.'

'Oh come on! Either there was a reason or there wasn't!'

'I think I might have killed myself. Spiritual if not physical death for certain.'

'George, you talk like an adolescent! What the hell is *spiritual death* when it's at home? How many ordinary people – employees in banks, insurance companies, supermarkets, factories, government offices – face "spiritual death" every day for 40 years without complaining? To put food on the table? Millions! Billions maybe! But that's not good enough for George Zafiris! Oh no, he's too delicate! He might get slightly bored! What crap you talk!'

'I was doing absolutely fine until the crisis.'

'Yes! And then? Disaster! Which is why, stupid, you find people taking jobs in banks! To protect them in times of crisis!'

'No one could have foreseen the storm that hit this country.'

'You didn't need to foresee it. Storms always come. Especially in Greece, where we do everything as badly as possible.'

George said nothing for a while. She had a point, of course. A good point. He had been running low on funds for five years now, and the past months had been worst of all. Somehow he had kept going, but he didn't know how much longer they could survive.

By the roadside they passed shops selling bathrooms, kitchens and bedroom furniture. Once these places were thriving, with shiny new jeeps and executive cars crowding the parking lots. Now they were deserted. The sudden, unexplained spending power of the Greek people, which had blazed like a comet through the 1990s and early 2000s, had just vanished into the dark. The wealth had been an illusion, borrowed not earned, conjured by fiscal magic out of the European hat.

Everyone had been too busy having a good time to ask who was paying or how. When the bill came it was enormous. More than 100 billion euros. Money the government could never raise except by further borrowing, or by such radical reform that it would require a complete re-education of the Greek people. The despair that settled on the country was worse than anything in living memory. Worse than the military junta of the 1960s, worse than the Nazi occupation and civil war. Worse even than the Asia Minor campaign, the 'great catastrophe' of 1922. With a monstrous debt to pay, and a budget deficit that grew bigger every year, things could only get worse.

'If you saw the crisis coming you should have warned me,' said George.

'If you had been sensible I wouldn't have needed to.'

Zoe had a way of cracking out these unanswerable lines. Their import was always the same: *you've failed!* George could not deny it; only plead that everyone makes mistakes and that forgiveness is one of the greatest of human accomplishments. As she accused him he felt like a child again, powerless, miserable and angry.

He was still trying to think of a suitable riposte when his phone rang. He wrestled it out of his pocket and passed it to Zoe. 'Can you see who that is?'

She glanced at it. 'Colonel Sotiriou.'

'Please answer and switch it to loudspeaker.'

She scowled. 'We're talking.'

'I know. We'll talk some more. But this is work.'

With an exasperated look she answered the phone.

'Zafiris?' barked Sotiriou. 'We've got your man, Wasim Khan.'

27

'How is he?'

'He's under guard.'

'Why?'

'In case he tries to escape.'

'He can't walk.'

'I know. But you'd be surprised. Desperation begets strength. Let's do this properly.'

'What does that mean?'

'Let the doctors do what they can. Then take him in, find out what's going on.'

'I promised he would have no dealings with the police.'

'You're not in a position to promise anything.'

'We agreed!'

'Not quite. You made a request which I cannot grant.'

'Don't you dare hit him with the usual bureaucratic shit.'

'I shall hit him, as you delicately put it, with any shit I please!'

'He's a witness, Colonel. A victim of a crime.'

'Exactly.'

'And there are more like him.'

'There are thousands like him all over Greece, Zafiris! All over the world. They are modern slaves.'

'I would expect you of all people, Colonel, to show some sympathy.'

'What the hell do you think I'm doing, Zafiris? You ruined my Sunday lunch, the whole afternoon has gone in telephone calls, and all for this Mr Wasim Bloody Khan!'

'I don't want you throwing the book at him.'

'Don't be stupid, Zafiris, it's not him I'm after. I want the people-smugglers, the gang-masters, the exploiters. If I can get at them through him, I shall.'

'I'd like to talk to him.'

'I'll have to think about that.'

'Why?'

'I don't want you interfering.'

'I just want to offer moral support. The guy's terrified.'

'I know. We can use that.'

'Use it? That's disgraceful.'

'Don't be so quick to condemn, Zafiris. Leave him to us.'

'I insist on seeing him!'

'You insist on nothing.'

The phone went dead.

Zoe interrupted his thoughts.

'So now you're going out of your way to help a penniless Pakistani? Is that how you hope to make money?'

'No,' said George. 'Of course not.'

'How are you going to pay the bills?'

'I don't know yet.'

'We're heading for bankruptcy, George! We're even running towards it! With our eyes open! It's a nightmare, a total nightmare!'

He stopped at a red light.

'Don't worry,' he said. 'Something will turn up.'

3

Haris Pezas phoned that evening to tell his weekly joke.

'A man was sitting in the café with a friend one day, and the friend asked, "Does your wife scream when she's making love?" "Scream?" says the husband. "You bet she does! I can hear her from over here!"'

Haris waited for the laugh.

'Is that it?' said George.

'I can hear her from over here!' Haris repeated the line, gurgling with laughter. 'From the café!'

George was not amused.

'OK Haris, we've done the joke. What next?'

'I just called to see how you are.'

'Lousy. You?'

'Same. What's cooking?'

'I rescued a Pakistani farm worker this afternoon and my wife is giving me hell for it. What are you up to?'

'Not much. We sold one electric kettle and four light bulbs this week. Total income 45 euros. A neighbour came round to borrow an onion and stayed two hours, telling us about her mother-in-law.'

'Sounds like a normal week in the provinces.'

'Right. Only this girl is Scottish.'

'Which girl?'

'The neighbour.'

'So?'

'I thought you might be interested.'

'Because she's Scottish?'

'Look, George, you said it sounds like a normal week in the provinces, and I'm telling you the girl is Scottish, so it's not quite a normal week, not in Corinth anyway. You get my point?'

'I get your point. I just wonder why you're making it.'

'The poor girl is isolated. No family, no friends, married to a spoilt little shit. She is tortured by his horrible mother.'

'What does she expect you to do about it?'

'Nothing. We just listened. Told her to be patient.'

'You think that will help?'

'It can't hurt.'

'Things only get worse in a marriage, Haris.'

'She needs a place to live. Do you happen to know anywhere?'

'What are you talking about? She has a home, doesn't she?'

'It's a place of torment.'

'I know the feeling.'

'She needs to escape.'

'Don't get involved, Haris! It will bring you grief.'

'I am involved.'

'You're having an affair?'

'No! I've promised to help. I feel sorry for her.'

'I don't know anyone with a spare room.'

'You must. All your rich friends.'

31

'They're a selfish lot. Very few Christian souls among them.'

'She's beautiful…'

'Even worse. No wife will let her near the house.'

'I'm only putting out the word, George.'

'Does she have children?'

'Two.'

'Any money?'

'A little.'

'What's her plan?'

'Just to get a breathing space, start thinking straight. Then see a lawyer about divorcing this idiot.'

'What's his problem?'

'He takes drugs, no job is good enough, he's an anarchist…'

'She should go home to Scotland.'

'They won't let her take the kids.'

'Sounds like a bloody nightmare. People get married too easily. They should be told, "Go into this with your eyes open. Only if you're sure. Fifty percent of you will get divorced." I can't help Haris, I have bad dreams of my own.'

'Just bear it in mind.'

'It's in there, my friend. Along with every other messed up life story in a very big collection.'

'Oh well. You listened at least.'

'You gave me no choice.'

'I really rang to ask if there's any work for me.'

George grunted. 'Nothing that pays.'

'We should put out some leaflets.'

'That didn't work last time.'

'Because we got busy.'

'We never had a single enquiry.'

'This time we might.'

'Or might not.'

'We lose nothing by trying. In fact the flow of energy seeks a return, like an electrical current.'

'Spare me the "energy" bullshit, Haris! Every superstitious, astrology-spouting, conspiracy-theory vegan fantasist goes on about *energy* the whole bloody time. I'm sick of it.'

'It's not bullshit, George! It works.'

'Grow up, Haris!'

'OK, buddy, I'm going to show you. Within one week you will be turning away business.'

George groaned. He was too tired to object.

4

The flyer arrived by email the next morning. In 1940s cinema poster style, it showed an evil-looking man sprinting down a city street gripping a lady's handbag. A short distance behind him a girl in a mini-skirt stood bewildered and helpless while indifferent onlookers walked by. 'WILL YOU CATCH HIM YOURSELF?' ran the caption. 'OR CALL IN A PROFESSIONAL?'

George picked up the phone. 'Listen, Haris, it's dramatic, it's eye-catching, in some ways it's brilliant, but that is not the kind of work we do.'

'I know,' said Haris, 'it's symbolic! To convey the idea of crime and the helplessness of the ordinary citizen.'

'Why not show a man setting off on a business trip, kissing his wife goodbye, with the caption, "Are you sure where he'll be spending the night?"'

Haris reacted indignantly. 'That's disgusting!'

'It's the reality.'

'You want to show the private detective as the destroyer of marriage?'

'No, but the fact is that adultery is our bread and butter.'

'Forget facts. This is advertising, George! We need to

be heroes.'

'I can't risk it, Haris. You know I could be prosecuted for trading under false pretences?'

'It's nothing. Let me take the risk. I tell you what: if we get into trouble – which we won't! – it's not you who's going to pay the bill for a lawyer, it's me.'

'All right. Do it. Print a thousand and we'll post them round the northern suburbs.'

Haris laughed.

'What's the joke?'

'You've just named the world capital of adultery.'

'So?'

'Even more reason not to mention it.'

Like many a simple idea, the flyer had immediate results, although not quite those George had in mind. To his surprise, Zoe was sprung from her usual indifference to his professional life and offered to walk round with him, pushing leaflets into letterboxes. They took two sides of a street, sharing the labour. The spring-loaded letterboxes had a way of pinching your fingers and tearing the flyers, and the residents gave you supercilious stares, as if you were a criminal or a parasite, tossing the leaflets aside or crumpling them without so much as a glance. Now George understood the blank, unresponding eyes of that urban underclass who roamed the suburbs every day with shopping trolleys full of free newspapers and take-away restaurant menus. It was a thankless slog, and you had to shut off your feelings to do it, but at least it was a shared slog. The icy atmosphere between George and Zoe began to thaw.

After two days they had done twenty streets in Kifissia.

There were hundreds more to do, a network spreading north into Politeia and Ekali, south into Maroussi, Halandri, Filothei and Psyhikó – without even starting on the streets of Kolonaki and Pangrati in the centre. It would take them weeks to get round them all, as well as thousands more leaflets. It struck George with sudden force what vast amounts of hidden wealth exist in Athens. Never openly acknowledged, not since the crisis of 2009 at least, and expensive German cars had given way to modest Japanese makes, but the money was still there. Still talking, but in a hushed voice.

Two days of leafletting left their legs weary and their fingers sore, but they had a sense of achievement, of having done something to fight the general apathy. Perhaps there was something to Haris' energy talk. The proof, however, would be in the response. They waited for the telephone to ring.

When it did ring, George was disappointed to hear the voice of Colonel Sotiriou.

'Over to you, Zafiris,' he barked. 'I can't get a damn thing out of this Wasim bugger. Either he's deaf or totally stupid, or a professional spy – which I find unlikely. It's like talking to a block of concrete.'

'Did you threaten him?'

'Not personally.'

'Your men did?'

'I don't encourage it.'

'In other words they did. What did they tell him?'

'He'd be on the next plane back to Karachi if he didn't talk.'

'That didn't scare him?'

'Apparently not. If he understood what they were saying.

36

Which is doubtful.'

'Did they offer any incentive?'

'Of course!'

'What?'

'He would *not* be on the next plane to Karachi.' Sotiriou laughed.

'Maybe he wants to go back?' said George, cutting him off. 'Maybe he's had enough of Greece? Have you considered that?'

'If he wants to go back we'll oblige him!'

'It's hardly a solution.'

'For him it could be perfect. And one less problem for us.'

'One more unsolved crime.'

'Stop arguing, Zafiris. Just go and see him.'

'Any chance of some money?'

'Not for this. No one wants to know. He's just a miserable immigrant. But I'll owe you a favour.'

'You owe me several already,' said George.

'Really? I thought you owed me.'

'No.'

Sotiriou made light of it. 'No matter. We'll find a way. Just get Mr Khan talking.'

5

The KAT hospital, like every public building in Athens, was an ants' nest of anxious humanity, swarming around doorways, calling out for attention, pressing with worried gaze the doctors who moved from room to room in their bloodstained white coats avoiding eye-contact. Relieved that he was not himself a patient, George waited for the lift to the third floor where, according to Colonel Sotiriou, Wasim Khan had been given a bed. The place was filthy. George wondered when hygiene had dropped off the list of hospital priorities. Plastic dispensers of anti-bacterial gel had been fixed to corridor walls, but the grimy finger marks around the lift's control buttons, the dust and brown smears on the floor, the stale air, told the unmistakable story of a battle being lost. Yet the squalor of the lift was nothing compared to the scene that was revealed by the opening doors. Beds jostling for space, their occupants staring hopelessly from their pillows or sleeping in postures of exhaustion, mouths open, heads flopped to one side. A flood of decaying body smells, blood, urine, sweat and faeces. Not a nurse or a doctor in sight. Only the wreckage of broken and disintegrating lives. Gagging at the foul air, George hurried through the ward, searching for Wasim.

He found him in a far corner. Over the puffy purple features of his face a grey veil seemed to have been poured like a layer of cement. His body was squeezed into an agonised foetal clench, as if he had been caught in the Medusa's petrifying gaze. Cautiously he touched one of Wasim's hands. Feeling its warmth, he pressed the triangle of muscle at the base of the thumb, gently at first, then hard. Wasim's eyelids fluttered and a grunt of fear burst from his cracked lips.

George asked how he was feeling.

'Who are you?' came the reply.

'My name is George. I've come to help you.'

Wasim's eyes widened in alarm. 'No! No help! Let me go!'

'I'm not keeping you,' said George. 'You're in hospital. You can leave as soon as you're strong again.'

'Police come!'

'You have no problem with the police.'

'I have bad problem with police.'

'There is no problem.'

'They ask papers. All time papers.'

'I can stop that. If you help, I can get papers for you.'

'No help! No papers…'

'Think about it.'

'You police?'

'No.' George considered explaining his relationship with the police, but it was hard enough to put into words at the best of times.

'I am not police,' he said, 'but I can help you. I'll get papers for you. It's very simple. I want to know who attacked you.'

Wasim did not seem to understand.

George mimed a series of blows and punches. 'Who did

39

that to you?'

The same uncomprehending look. George tried again, pointing to Wasim's bruised face and arms. There was no reaction.

He tried a different approach.

'You were working in the fields?'

'I work,' said Wasim.

'Who was your boss? Who paid you?'

'Nobody pay me!'

'That can't be true. Somebody paid you. Who?'

'Nobody pay me!' Wasim insisted.

'But you were working?'

'I work! Long time!'

'No pay?'

'No pay.'

'Why no pay? Maybe the man who is going to pay…'

'My boss.'

'Yes! Who is that?'

No reply.

'Did your boss attack you?'

'His friend.'

'I need names, Wasim! Give me their names!'

'No.'

'Why not?'

'They kill me.'

'Where are your friends, Wasim?'

'My friends run away.'

'Where?'

'Other place.'

'Where? Athens? Rafina? Spata?'

'Away.'

'This is hopeless! Give me some names!'

Wasim sighed. His eyes closed heavily. His energy was all gone.

A muffled trio of syllables, sluggish and thick, drifted out of his mouth. Antoni? Manolis? Karoly? Only the vowels were recognisable. The consonants in between were anyone's guess.

George waited a few minutes to let Wasim recover. His breathing, already shallow and slow, seemed to dwindle, growing fainter and fainter, until George was no longer sure that he could see any movement at all. George shook him, tweaked his ear, even poured a trickle of cold water on his face. In sudden alarm, he grabbed Wasim's left wrist and felt for a pulse. Ten seconds. Fifteen. Twenty-five. Nothing. Wasim was far away, beyond reach.

George laid Wasim's hand down gently on the bed. Sorrow gripped his heart. Instead of healing in hospital, Wasim had been left to deteriorate. The life had been drained out of him. Why was that? Medical neglect? Fear? Loss of the will to live? Beaten and terrorised out of him?

Had the police contributed to that?

In anger he called Colonel Sotiriou.

'I don't know what your men did to him,' he said bitterly, 'but he's no good to anyone now.'

'What are you talking about, Zafiris?'

'Wasim!'

'What's happened?'

'He's dead.'

'How do you know?'

'I'm standing next to him.'

'You've checked his pulse?'

'Of course!'

Sotiriou swore.

'This is now a murder case,' said George.

'I could quarrel with that.'

'Why? To cover for your men?'

'Don't be stupid, Zafiris.'

'I'm serious.'

'My men know what they're doing.'

'I very much doubt that. Let's see what the doctors say.'

There was a heavy pause. The Colonel spoke solemnly. 'Zafiris, don't be officious. Any trouble you cause will damage our relationship.'

'Don't you dare threaten me!'

'That's not a threat.'

'Sounds like a threat to me!'

'Think of it as… a prophecy. The poor man's life is over. You can't bring him back. Let's work together, to achieve what we can.'

'I hear the violins playing, Colonel, but I don't like the tune.'

'There are many worse sounds, Zafiris!'

'Not to me, Colonel. I've always thought of you as a decent man.'

'You're jumping to conclusions, as you always do. You need to get out of there, and fast. Walk out of the hospital right now. Normal speed, calm and easy. Don't speak to anyone. Act as if nothing has happened. I'll call you.'

'I never thought I'd hear you talk like that,' said George.

'Will you please just do it?'

'I'll do what I think right. Damn you and your men!'
George ended the call.

He stayed where he was contemplating the wretched figure on
the bed, the sheet off one skinny shoulder, the face fixed in a
grimace of pained surprise. With a glance around him, George
searched the bedside table, found a rolled-up pair of trousers
with a mobile phone and a scrap of paper in one pocket. He
palmed them swiftly and turned to go. After a few steps, on
impulse, he turned again and snapped a couple of pictures of
Wasim with his phone. Miserable, desolate shots – possibly
evidence of some kind.

He hurried out, wondering how many hours or even days it
would be before anyone noticed that the patient had died.

6

Back home in Aristotle Street, George found Zoe in an energetic mood.

'I've been thinking, George. People owe you money. Why don't you collect it?'

'Who?'

'Past clients. You always complain about them. I don't know their names.'

George shuddered at the memory. 'I know who you're thinking of. Anna Kenteri, who's in prison, and Byron Kakridis, who's too powerful to pursue. I won't get anything from them.'

'You don't even try.'

'I've tried.'

'Try again.'

'OK,' he said to close the conversation, 'I'll try again.'

Zoe persisted. 'How much do they owe you?'

'Anna Kenteri about two thousand. Kakridis five, maybe six.'

'That would solve our problems!'

'If we could get the money. But we can't.'

'You need a lawyer.'

'No doubt. And who is going to pay the bill?'

'You'll pay. Out of the proceeds.'

'You know how long it takes to go through the courts?'

'Of course. It's terrible. But no one likes to be threatened with legal action. And you have every right. Frighten them at least. Put some pressure. You can't just let them get away with it!'

'That's what they're used to.'

'You have a duty too. If you don't stand up for justice, what are the ordinary Greeks going to do, who don't have your knowledge, your connections?'

'I'll talk to Yiannis.'

'Make sure you do. He's doing well. He'll do it on credit, I'm sure.'

'I'll call him now,' said George, wanting more than ever to escape Zoe's grilling.

She was right, of course. He was avoiding the problem. But ten years of legal battles was not a happy prospect, dealing not so much with confrontations as evasions, delays, strikes, postponements, accidents, illness (real and invented) and the immense, immovable institutional inertia of state officials, with their logjams of documents, signatures, permits, stamps, authentications and powers of attorney, their visceral hostility to the public, their arrogance, narrow-mindedness, laziness and complete absence of a sense of duty. A nightmare lay before him. Was that worth 7,000 euros? Would he not spend ten times that amount in wasted life and energy?

Yiannis Koroneos was an old schoolfriend. He was a studious, scholarly, thoughtful man who acted as George's lawyer

45

whenever the need arose, and had the great virtue of never sending in a bill. In pre-crisis days George used to treat him to a night out at the opera or dinner at a good taverna, but Yiannis was too busy now and George too short of money. They seldom met.

'You disappeared,' said Yiannis. 'Where have you been?'

'In the swamp. Struggling.'

'That's where I've been too. I didn't see you.'

'It's a big place.'

'Damn right it is, and getting bigger. How can I help?'

George outlined the problem.

'Can you give me names?'

'Sure. Anna Kenteri commissioned me to find her sister's killer.'

'Did you succeed?'

'I did.'

'So why didn't she pay?'

'First, because it wasn't the person she wanted it to be. Second because when she found out who it was, she went out and shot him. She's in prison now.'

'That shouldn't stop her paying. Is there any dispute about the debt?'

'No, just enormous anger. She was convinced it was her sister's husband.'

'You did your job.'

'Exactly.'

'What about the other one?'

'That's more difficult. Byron Kakridis.'

'The Minister? Ex-PASOK, now Syriza?'

'Exactly.'

'What did you do for him?'

'I followed his wife, at his request, and found out she was having an affair with another politician.'

'He was displeased, I take it?'

'Very.'

'He definitely commissioned you?'

'Of course.'

'Anything in writing?'

'No.'

'With either case?'

'I might have sent a few emails with interim reports.'

'I'll need copies of those. You don't issue contracts?'

'Very rarely.'

'Why not?'

'It's tricky. There's a lot of trust and confidentiality involved. Anything on paper can get into the wrong hands…'

'Of course. But with a good contract and payments in advance, you can avoid this kind of mess.'

'They give me all kinds of excuses. Especially now. People losing 30–40% of their purchasing power, of their income…'

'You need to turn those clients away.'

'And run short of work? No thanks!'

'George…' The lawyer sounded suddenly weary. 'We're all going through difficult times. I can only help you if you help yourself.'

'I understand,' said George. 'I'll do as you say.'

'You won't regret it.'

'Meanwhile, how can you help?'

'I'm not sure I can. You know the French saying, *pourquoi chercher midi à quatorze heures?* Don't look for noon at two o'clock. The opportunity has gone.'

'Oh come on, Yianni, this is just chasing debt. Half the country's doing it!'

'Because they failed to take precautions.'

'OK, I failed! I admit it. What now?'

'I can send letters, I suppose.'

'Will that work?'

'No.'

'So why do it?'

'To establish the claim.'

'Then what?'

'I can follow them up.'

'Apply to the courts?'

'If necessary. I can also go and see these people. But it all takes time and money.'

'What leverage do you have?'

'Argue the case calmly, forcefully, with the threat of legal action.'

'Are there any other routes?'

'Of course, but you don't need a lawyer for those.'

'Who do I need?'

Yiannis laughed. 'I can't possibly tell you that.'

'You mean heavies?'

'I'm not saying any more.'

'OK,' said George. 'Just write the letters.'

7

By taking action – any action – George soon felt better. His confidence returned, and with it a sense of how little of it was left after seven years of crisis. Like many Athenians he had grown accustomed to a life without hope. He was even beginning to find it comfortable. It was so simple to say no to everything – all luxuries, projects, ideas, holidays, novelties – anything at all that cost money. And what did not? But it went against his instincts.

Austerity! Thrift! It was forcibly recommended by the European Union, the World Bank and the International Monetary Fund, not to mention centuries of proverbs and so-called common sense. It had a literal-minded logic. Spend less and you have more! A pity it was only half-true, working well enough in cases of foolish extravagance but fatally in others. As one Greek politician had put it in a rare moment of eloquence, *If you starve the cow it won't give you any milk.*

Reducing his commitments to zero would also destroy all prospect of recovery. He had to keep going, uphill as it was, however low his energy and hope. Without work and money coming in, his life would quickly fall apart. Zoe would leave him, they would be forced to sell the flat, and with half the meagre proceeds he would have no choice but to move to the provinces, some remote and dreary place of exile from which there would be no return.

A week passed, and he waited. No response to his lawyer's letters, no follow-up from the flyers. George spent his time reading and walking. He read a book that Nick had brought him on his last visit: *Stasiland.* With its horrifying stories about the secret police in East Germany, it made him feel that even in crisis-poisoned Greece life was not so bad. At least you were free to think and suffer in your own way.

He would call in every morning at the Café Agamemnon for a cup of coffee. Politics was always on the agenda here, sometimes in discussion with Dimitri alone, sometimes with other customers venting their anger or ranting in favour of one conspiracy theory or another.

There were plenty to choose from:

'Capitalism's a racket. Europe's a racket. The Americans are spraying us with tranquillisers from high-flying surveillance aircraft. A secret club of billionaires is rigging the markets, financing Putin and Trump. Greece is a pawn in their cynical game. The Aegean has huge reserves of oil, but the big players want it. The Greek mountains are full of gold, but foreigners are mining it. Our ancient works of art earn millions of euros for the countries that stole them – England, France, Germany, America – but we see none of it. The Germans destroyed our country in the 1940s and never paid a cent in reparations; and they say we owe them money! We gave the world civilisation: when will the world give something back?'

George was sick of hearing these arguments. From time to

time he would react. 'These theories are bullshit. Excuses for our failure. We have borrowed billions and we have to pay it back. Simple as that.'

Dimitri usually agreed with him, but since his café sat on the border between Kolonaki and Exarchia, with customers from right and left, he was careful to hedge his bets.

'Fair enough, Mr George. I have no quarrel with you. But still, something doesn't add up!'

What certainly did not add up was the household accounts. Zoe came to him one evening and handed him a piece of paper. 'These are the things we could sell,' she said. 'If anyone will buy them.'

Top of the list was his red Alfa Romeo Spider. He knew it would be. It was his favourite possession, a reminder of the good old days when money was plentiful and cares far-distant.

'I'd rather sell my body on the streets than part with that,' he said.

'It's just a car!'

'My body's just a body.'

She laughed.

'It has sentimental value,' he said.

'Don't you think my jewels have sentimental value too?'

'Of course. We should only sell what we can bear to part with.'

'No. We should sell what makes us money. You sell the Alfa, I'll sell my jewellery. It's a deal.'

'Can we give it a few days?'

'Why?'

'Maybe some work will come up.'
'It had better. I'll give you 48 hours.'

The next day, forced into action, George printed more flyers and was out on the streets of Kolonaki stuffing letterboxes. The weather was bright, with that brilliant Athenian winter sunshine that opens wild flowers and beckons bees and butterflies from their cold-weather quarters. Haris' words about energy echoed in his head as he walked. The idea did not seem so nonsensical now. Taking the first step, the journey was already shorter. The start, as the proverb goes, is half the task.

As if triggered by some unconscious impulse, his phone rang. An unknown number.

'Hello, Mr Zafiris?'

'That's me.'

'It's Olli.'

'Olli?'

'Olli Papaspirou. We met at lunch the other Sunday, by the sea. I'm with Pandelís.'

'Olli, *kalimera*. What can I do for you?'

'You heard about the burglary?'

'Where?'

'At my parents' house.'

'No one told me. When was that?'

'Last Saturday.'

'Did they lose much?'

'A lot.'

'Sorry to hear it. I presume your parents have an alarm?'

'My father's stuck in the past. He says Greece is a country without crime.'

'He should install an alarm at once.'

'I keep telling him.'

There was a pause. Then, with a hint of embarrassment, 'Mr Zafiris, I rang to ask if you can do something for me.'

'What would that be?'

'You're a private investigator?'

'Correct.'

'Can you maybe try to help me find something that was stolen?'

'What?'

'Some jewellery.'

'I can try. It won't be easy.'

'I'm totally stuck. I don't even know where to begin.'

'It's not my field,' said George. 'But my first recommendation is to consult a specialist.'

'That's what you are, surely?'

'There are people who work entirely in the underground gem trade.'

'Do you know where to find those people?'

'A couple of phone calls will do it.'

'It would be so great if you could help me!'

'You realise it will cost?'

'Oh?' She sounded surprised. 'How much?'

'I charge 200 euros a day plus expenses – and that's a crisis special price; it was 300 last year – then there's the specialist, who may work on a percentage or a flat fee.'

'How much would that be?'

'3,000 at a guess. Maybe more depending on the value of the item.'

Olli said nothing for a while.

'Changed your mind?' said George.

'No. It's just… as you're *family*…'

'The specialist isn't family.'

'I guess not. What about your price?'

'It's as low as it can go.'

'OK. Let me think.'

'Do your parents know you've called me?'

Her voice was suddenly hostile. 'Why do you ask?'

'I presume it's your mother's jewellery.'

'Not entirely.'

'What do you mean?'

'There's something of mine in there.'

'Something valuable?'

'Yes.'

'Can you be more specific?'

'A diamond necklace.'

'Real diamonds?'

'Of course!'

'OK. Do you have an idea of the value?'

'I do.'

'Give me a figure.'

'100,000.'

George gave a start. 'Are you sure?'

'I'm sure.'

'Can I ask where you bought this necklace?'

'I didn't. It was an engagement present. From Pandelís.'

'Nice present.'

'Absolutely.'

'Does he know it's gone?'

'No.'

'Why don't you tell him?'

'I'm afraid of his reaction.'

'What do you think that will be?'

'He'll go crazy.'

'You think he'll blame you?'

'Of course.'

'Is it your fault the necklace was stolen?'

She hesitated before answering. 'Not really.'

'You sound uncertain.'

'Maybe a bit my fault.'

'How?'

'I kept it in my bedside table. It should have been in the safe.'

'It's easy to say that now.'

'He *told* me to keep it in the safe. He actually told me! And I promised I would. But I wanted it near me. I wanted to touch it… I put it on at night sometimes, just to enjoy it. God, how stupid I am!'

'Listen, Olli, you've done what anybody else would have done. It's bad luck. Pandelís will understand.'

'No, he won't. He'll go mad. He's so precise about every-thing. So methodical. He won't even begin to understand. He'll say, "You promised to keep it in the safe. We had an agreement. You disregarded that!"'

'He may say that, but in the end he'll forgive you. He has to. Lesson number one in married life.'

'You don't know what he's like. He could call off our engagement over this. That's what scares me most.'

'In that case you'll be well rid of him.'

'Mr Zafiris! How can you say that? I love him!'

'I'm sure you do. But if he's prepared to ditch you for a necklace, you have to wonder how much he loves you.'

'Of course he loves me!'

'Then you have nothing to worry about.'

George realised this was going in the wrong direction. He was talking himself out of a job.

'Listen,' he said, 'I'm going to be very clear. Today is the time to act. Stolen jewellery gets broken up quickly to prevent recognition. If you really want that necklace back, and you can lay your hands on 5000 euros, decide now and we're in business.'

'You said 3,000!'

'That's just for the specialist. He may want more. There's my fee too, plus expenses.'

'Still…'

'It's yes or no!'

'Maybe we could meet for a coffee? And discuss it?'

'Coffee's fine, Olli, but bring the money. I'm telling you straight so you know. It has to be like this. No money, no action.'

'No family discount?'

'It's built in.'

'I thought at least you might…'

'No!'

'All right,' she said reluctantly. 'I'll see what I can do.'

8

George said nothing to Zoe about the call from Olli, but he could not stop thinking about it. A diamond necklace worth €100,000… Where did Pandelís get hold of money like that? Were Stelios and Maria so rich? He asked himself what he actually knew about them, and it was pitifully little. Tax and construction. Construction and tax. Nothing more. What kind of construction? Houses? Roads? Offices? Bridges? He hadn't the faintest idea.

Over a bowl of chick pea soup in the kitchen with Zoe he tried indirectly to find out more.

'I've been wondering what Nick would do if he worked for Stelios,' he said.

'That's up to Stelios.'

'Of course. But if Nick were to mention a part of the business that he's interested in, it would show some initiative.'

'Initiative is one thing, good manners is another. You should have thought about all this when you were so rude to Stelios at lunch.'

'I wasn't rude.'

'You most certainly were!'

'If so it was not intentional.'

'You knew what you were doing! You called him boring.'

'So he is.'

'Oh please, George, we've been through this! Nick needs a job. Your opinion of Stelios is irrelevant!'

'I wish I knew what it is they do. How they make their money.'

'What difference does it make? This isn't about you and what you know.'

'Of course.'

'It's about Nick.'

'All right,' said George, trying to be patient. 'Look at it this way. Nick's studying to be a mechanical engineer. The jobs he can go for typically are in shipping, aviation, transport, maybe electricity. What have Stelios and Maria to do with any of that?'

'I have no idea. But *they* know! And if they need engineers, and they like Nick, and you stop insulting them, they might just offer him a job!'

'Can't you tell me what they do? In case Nick asks?'

'You know what they do. Construction. Maria has her day job at the tax office, but I know she helps the firm in her spare time.'

'That's all you know?'

'They don't discuss business affairs with me, and I certainly don't ask.'

'They do pretty well though?'

'They certainly do.'

'I wonder if they build roads, or houses, or office blocks…'

Zoe pressed her hands to the sides of her head. 'George, I can't bear it!'

'OK,' he said. 'I get the point.'

Olli telephoned later that evening to say she had the money. She wanted to meet the next day. The question was where. It had to be discreet, away from everyone's home districts. George suggested a place on the northern edge of the city, Agios Stefanos, known (if it was known at all) chiefly for its used car dealers. He told Zoe he was going out there to sell the Alfa. She looked pleased.

'At last,' she said coldly. 'A moment of realism.'

Next morning he collected his treasure from the garage and took the National Road to the North. Out past Lykovrisi, Kifissia, Varibobi, the sun angled across the road in slanting shafts of dusty gold. He was working again. And driving the Alfa. It felt good.

He turned off the highway for Agios Stefanos and followed its ribbon of a main street to a Mitsubishi garage, where he pulled in and parked among pick-up trucks and urban jeeps. He pushed through the glass doors of the showroom and greeted the young salesman, Christoforos, whom he knew slightly.

'Is the boss about?'

'He's with a client, Mr Zafiris. He's away for the day. Can I help?'

'I want to sell my Alfa. Ask him to take a look, would you?' He placed the key in the centre of the desk.

'What price are you looking for?'

'High as possible. She's a great machine, top condition.'

'Full service, genuine parts?'

'Low mileage too.'

'Year?'

'1982.'

59

'The year I was born! You know something, I wouldn't mind it myself.'

'So make me an offer.'

'As soon as I can get someone to sit at this desk I'll take her for a spin. I love the old Alfas! Such a delicate design! Not like these bloody battleships people want today.'

'Ask the boss to take a look. I'll come back tomorrow.'

George walked 150 metres down the road to 'Coffee Century', one of a series of characterless establishments that had invaded Athens in the past ten years, wiping out the old neighbourhood *kafeneio* where men, and only men, sat playing *tavli* and talking politics all day. Greek coffee, in its little white cup, had been hustled off the menu by more fashionable Italian and American imports with five times more liquid and ten times less taste. Like the cigarettes that were once smoked here in such suicidal quantities – Papastratos No 1, Karelia, Pallas, Ethnos, Aroma, Old Navy, Club, Santé, Rex – the old cafés had disappeared. No one seemed to regret their going, passively accepting the bland new substitutes without a word. George met the eye of the weary employee behind the counter, ordered a double espresso and sat down. The place was empty apart from a uniformed van driver staring out at the road with a blank gaze. The radio, playing too loud, completed the job of destroying the atmosphere with a mixture of pop songs and advertisements for supermarkets and mobile phones. A wave of anger and disgust rose up in him at the thought of what had happened to his city, his culture, his country. They had borrowed money to buy into the American way of life, trash their past, and live in unpayable debt. He felt like an animal with its legs caught in a trap.

'You look happy!'

He glanced up.

'Olli. Sorry, I was miles away.'

She leaned forward to kiss him, once on each cheek, in a dense cloud of black hair and floral perfume.

'What will you have?'

'Cappuccino.'

The man at the counter, perking up at the sight of Olli, offered to bring it over.

George sat down again, thinking how much livelier she looked than the last time he had seen her, when she had seemed sunk in her rôle as future daughter-in-law. She carried a force with her now, even as she stirred sugar into her coffee, a dynamism and energy.

'Thanks for coming out,' she said. 'It means a lot to me.'

'I hope I can help.'

She smiled. 'I'm sure you can. I feel totally isolated.'

'Tell your parents and Pandelís. That will improve things.'

'I can't tell them. Not yet. Not until I've tried everything.'

'This may not work,' he said.

'We have to try.'

'Have you seen the police?'

She groaned. 'Oh yes. Fingerprints, statements. It's a formality for them. They're bored.'

'It's an act.'

'I don't think so.'

'Some police really care about their work.'

'Not the ones I met! They sit around, talking on their phones, drinking coffee, complaining about their shifts. Not for a moment did they show any interest in my case.'

'They didn't perk up when you walked in?'

She shrugged this off. 'Oh yes, they *flirted*. In their stupid way.'

'What do you mean?'

'Oh, you know. They look lazy and bored. They think it's cool. I think it's brainless. Anyway they clearly don't give a damn about their work.'

'OK. Let's see what they come up with. Meanwhile do you have a picture of the necklace?'

She took a smartphone from her bag and flicked through its photos. George sipped his coffee.

'There,' she said, and turned the screen towards him. There was a photo of an exquisite contemporary diamond necklace, sparkling around the neck of a girl in a skimpy bikini. The girl was Olli.

'Did you show that to the police?' asked George.

'They didn't ask for a picture.'

'It's pretty distracting.'

She laughed. 'We were doing glamour shots.'

'Who's "we"?'

'Me and a girlfriend.'

George was bemused. 'Well, that's certainly glamorous. But I wouldn't use it for identification purposes.'

'It got your attention.'

'I can't show it to a jewellery expert.'

'Why not?'

He threw up his hands. 'It should be obvious.'

'I'll send it to you,' she said. 'And you can crop it. What's your email address?'

George bridled. 'I can't keep that picture on my phone. If Zoe saw it…'

Olli laughed. 'It's not as if you can see anything.'

'You can see quite enough.'

'It's meant as a tease.'

'Just crop it for me, will you? I don't want your face or anything below the shoulders. And if I were you I wouldn't flash that around. Men are animals.'

'Tell me about it!'

George wrote down his email address.

'I've brought the money,' she said.

'Good.'

'Do you want it all now?'

'I've explained why it's necessary.'

She rummaged in her bag again and pulled out an envelope. 'It's all there.'

George slipped it into his pocket.

'Won't you count it?'

'Later,' he said. 'If it's short I won't start work.'

She seemed amused. 'Tough guy, eh?'

'Just practical.'

She sipped her coffee, still amused. Her phone rang. She glanced at it and rejected the call.

'Do you want to see the scene of the crime?' she asked.

'Not particularly.'

'Why not?'

'You want me to get this necklace back. What's the scene of the crime got to do with it?'

'I don't know. Perhaps the style of the burglary will tell you something important. Or maybe you'll find fingerprints where

63

the police didn't.'

'No. Let me get this photo to the specialist. We have to work fast, before the diamonds are sold. It may be too late.'

'I understand. But I still think you should see where it happened.'

'Maybe later. That's really a separate job. For now we must concentrate on what we have to do. Nothing else.'

'I think my father should talk to you about security.'

'Agreed.'

'I could tell him you'll come round?'

'Will he see me?'

'If I tell him to he will.'

'You have him well trained, then?'

'Oh yes!'

'Where do you live?'

'Psyhikó. Iasemión 12.'

'Shall we say tomorrow afternoon? About four?'

'Perfect. What else do you need?'

'Nothing.' He stood up. 'I must go.'

'So brief?'

'I want to get moving.'

She smiled, a lightning flash in her dark eyes.

George left the café, wondering if her flirting was intentional. And, if it was, what she was hoping to gain.

9

Spyros Lagos had an office on the first floor of a building on Trikoupi Street, near the Olympia Theatre. A show business agent and a tour operator shared the landing, which was dingy and smelt of cigarette smoke. When the door opened, George found himself standing in a narrow strip of floor between the desk and the door. He was not invited to sit down, possibly because there was no spare chair.

The baize-covered desk was adorned with a green-shaded lamp and a jeweller's magnifying glass. Lagos, a heavily built man in his seventies, looked up at him with melancholy, liquid eyes.

George handed him the photograph of Olli's necklace, trimmed of her face and voluptuous body. 'That's a very expensive item,' he said lugubriously. 'It won't be cheap to get it back.'

He seemed well used to imparting bad news.

'How much, approximately?'

Instead of replying, Lagos looked George up and down.

'Have they offered a reward?'

'No,' said George.

'It might help.'

'I'll pass it on. How much will it cost to get this back?'

Lagos did not move a muscle. He stared at the photo with the fixity of a corpse.

'How much –'

'I heard you.' Still staring straight ahead, he said, 'It's an Italian design. Bulgari, I would guess. Retail price 80,000 to 120,000 euros. Am I right?'

'Spot on.'

'Broken down of course, the stones are worth much less. They'll fetch 15 or 20. That's the price you need to offer.'

'Can you find the necklace?'

The gloomy expression deepened. 'That's the tricky part.'

'I'd like you to make some enquiries.'

Lagos frowned. 'It's not so simple.'

He indicated the photo. 'Can I keep this?'

'Go ahead.'

George waited. Thoughts seemed to move very slowly through the old man's brain.

'Do you think –'

'There are private sessions,' said Lagos. 'Secret markets for stolen jewellery. You go by invitation and bid for items. These diamonds might turn up. It's your only chance. But it costs.'

'How much?'

'3,000 euros just to get through the door.'

'And if you don't find what you came for?'

'Then you have a chance to make your money back by buying something else.'

'I'm not interested in anything else.'

'That is unfortunate.'

'No refunds?'

'No refunds.'

'It sounds like a racket.'

'It's a very special opportunity. That's all I can say.'

'It still sounds like a racket.'

A glimmer of optimism flickered in the sad eyes. 'You can put the word out a few days before the market. This will increase your chances.'

'Still sounds risky.'

'It's the only way.'

'Can you put out the word?'

Lagos paused before replying. 'I can arrange it,' he said. 'But I'll need 3,000 down, plus 500 for myself.'

'I don't like it.'

'No one likes it. But that's the system.'

'You mentioned a reward? Paid when the goods are returned, not before?'

Lagos remained impassive. 'We're dealing with criminals, Mr Zafiris, not gentlemen.'

'Which are you?'

A weary sigh, and the ghost of a smile. 'I am the go-between. The divided man, who deals with both.'

George considered the divided man. He had the pendulous cheeks and dewlap of a Bassett hound, with plump, clean-shaven, greyish-yellow skin. Not much hair remained on his head, just a few strands slicked back across the scalp, which was smooth and mottled. His hands were manicured, supple and strong. There was nothing in his manner or appearance that gave a clue to the man's ethics. He could be a crook or a decent sort. Or, as he implied himself, something in between.

'When is the next of these private markets?'

'Three days from now.'

'Could we put out the word?'

'Of course.'

'I don't want to spend 3,500 euros for nothing.'

'Obviously.'

George remained uncertain. Lagos was a strange, troglo-dytic creature, but personally recommended. Reputedly the best of a dodgy lot.

'How often do you find what you're looking for, Mr Lagos?'

'Often enough. I'm in business, aren't I?'

'Do you have any references?'

'References?'

'From satisfied clients?'

'I'm not on Trip Advisor.'

George laughed.

'If we can't find your necklace we'll find something else. You won't lose out.'

'No thanks. We're not interested in buying stolen goods.'

A large hand pushed the photograph back across the desk. 'Good luck with it. If you change your mind let me know.'

George walked out onto Trikoupi Street, making an effort to clear his thoughts. This private market was absurdly risky, but what alternative did he have? They might try offering a reward, but who to? How would it be publicised? He decided to call Olli.

'Mr Zafiris!' she cried. 'That is totally amazing! I was just about to call you.'

'Why?'

'I've just had the most incredible conversation with a local shopkeeper. Apparently there was a whole series of burglaries in the neighbourhood last weekend. What's more, it's well known who did them!'

'Oh yes? Who?'

'A pair of Albanian twins. They used to work in the circus.'

'Do we know their names?'

'He didn't tell me that. But the police know them well. Every few years these guys do a sweep through the area. They get into the most amazingly difficult places, using their circus skills. They've been caught once or twice, served time in prison, then they get out for good behaviour and do it all over again!'

'You talk as if you admire them.'

'Well they're unusual, you have to admit!'

'Have you passed this on to the police?'

'Not yet. You'd think the cops might figure this out for themselves.'

'Don't overestimate their intelligence. Or their time.'

'OK,' she said. 'That's useful to know. I suppose they are quite busy. Making coffee and so on.'

George described his dilemma about Mr Lagos, and asked her what she wanted to do. But she would not decide. Instead she asked what he would do. He in turn refused to say. When she objected, he explained that it all depended on how desperate she was to retrieve the diamonds.

'It's my whole life with Pandelís,' she said.

'In that case your decision is clear. Pay Mr Lagos and hope for the best.'

'Is that the only way?'

'No. The simplest.'

'Or…? Is there an alternative?'

'We can try to find the Albanians instead.'

'How hard will that be?'

'I don't know. Nor do I know if they still have the necklace, or if they'll be willing to return it. Or under what conditions.'

She said nothing.

'Think about it,' he said, 'and call me. But don't leave it too long.'

'I don't know how to do that! Thinking is not my strong point.'

'You probably don't use pen and paper, do you?'

'Not much.'

'Well find some, and make a list of what each course of action will involve. Things to be done, by me or others, and their costs, but especially what *you* have to do, which in my view must include speaking openly and frankly to Pandelís.'

'Why don't you just tell me what to do, Mr Zafiris? You're the expert!'

'I'm in the dark as much as you are.'

'What's your gut feeling?'

'My gut feeling,' said George, 'is as unreliable as anybody else's. Accurate one day, hopeless the next.'

'Don't play games with me, Mr Zafiris. This is driving me nuts! Please just tell me what *you* would do.'

George drew breath and patiently spelled out his thoughts. 'Those diamonds are not mine, Olli, my future happiness doesn't depend on them, and I would advise you not to let yours depend on them either. I don't like putting cash into the criminal economy, especially with no guarantee of a return.

So I would not give 3,500 euros to Mr Lagos, I would do everything in my power to meet the Albanians.'

'Bravo!' said Olli. 'That's what I'm going to do.'

'Are you not at least going to think about it?'

'No! I'm paying you to do that for me.'

'Really?' said George. 'You're taking a big risk.'

'I don't think so.'

'OK. You want me to find the Albanians?'

'Yes!'

'It will take time and money.'

'It's OK.'

'So when can I come to Psyhikó and inspect the scene of the crime?'

'I thought you didn't want to do that.'

'I've changed my mind.'

'May I know why?'

'I've seen Lagos now; we're going down a different road. I need information. Clues. Details. All that physical stuff that never gets into a report.'

'About 5 pm?'

'See you then.'

10

Colonel Sotiriou sat uneasily at his desk, scattering black looks.

'I'm sorry to bother you,' said George, 'but I was passing, so I…'

'You were passing! If I spoke to every private detective who was "passing", do you know how much work I would do? None!'

'Exactly! I sympathise. But it's so difficult to get you on the phone that I thought I would give myself the pleasure of seeing you in person.'

'Here I am. Take what pleasure you can. But get on with it. I'm busy.'

George asked if he knew anything of the housebreaking circus acrobats. The Colonel said he did not. Would it be possible, George politely inquired, to put out a word among his colleagues? The Colonel asked why. George explained about the necklace. The Colonel interrupted him to point out that it did not appear to be a violent crime and was not therefore a matter for his department. George agreed, but hoped that the Colonel might be able to exploit his wider network of police contacts in order to solve a number of crimes which, although not violent, were nevertheless police business. Or should be. Sotiriou winced.

'You must think I have nothing better to do.'

'Far from it, Colonel. But you get things done. You're a man to rely on. A rarity in our country of talkers.'

'Get out,' said Sotiriou. 'If there's one thing I hate, it's bullshit flattery.'

'This is not bullshit.'

'It is, and you know it very well!'

'You'll help me?'

The Colonel waved him away. 'Call me tomorrow.'

George left the police building in a good mood. As brush-offs from the Colonel went, this was mild. It promised well.

He flagged down a taxi on Leoforos Alexandras and asked to be taken to the Mistubishi garage in Agios Stefanos.

The boss, Thanasis, waved him in from a desk smothered in papers. A smell of motor oil hung in the air.

'Boy, am I glad to see you! Get me out of this prison!' He spread his hands across the sea of papers in a gesture of despair. 'What's all this? Tax rules! New ones to supplement the ones they sent last month. Which modified the rules from the month before that. The government is terrified in case we make any profit. Bastards!'

George said, 'I've come to pick up my Alfa. Did you take a look?'

'I did. Lovely car, George, but don't sell her now.'

'How much would I get?'

'A dealer might offer you 3,000 max.'

'And sell it for what? Six?'

'If he's lucky. More like four.'

'What can you offer?

'3,500. As you're a friend.'

George was appalled. 'It's hardly worth it.'

'You need the cash?'

'Badly.'

'Then take the hit and forget about it as soon as you can.'

'I feel like the car is a part of me.'

Thanasis smiled. 'These are evil times, George. We're all saying goodbye to things we love.'

George said, 'I'll have to think about it. Maybe sell it abroad. I'm sure I'd get more in Italy.'

'Things aren't much better there. This single European currency was a disaster from the beginning. It hits the south harder than the north.'

'Because the south is disorganised.'

'Still, it's not exactly fair.'

'Don't fool yourself, Thanasi. We're in a mess because we can't sort ourselves out. Maybe don't even want to. Don't blame the north.'

'I want to blame somebody! I didn't ask to be buried alive in regulations! I'd like to spend a few minutes of my life actually *living*, wouldn't you?'

'It would be really good.'

George left his friend to wrestle with the tax regulations and found Christoforos on the way out.

'What did he offer you?' asked the young man in a whisper.

'3,500. Can you do any better than that?'

'Let me check. I'm not exactly rolling in cash.'

George picked up the key and left the building. As he

started the engine, felt its rasping blast, and steered the car softly into the traffic, he wondered how he could let this go for a handful of euros.

Down at Faros he turned into the lunatic maze of one-way streets that is Old Psyhikó. Iasemión, the street of the jasmines, was a relatively easy one to find, but you had to come in from the south. If you attempted it from the north you were forced away, with no more than a glimpse of its leafy end, into a bewildering labyrinth of left and right hand turns that always brought you out a good kilometre away, on the far side of the suburb, at a roundabout in front of the Arsakio school where you had to choose between five exits, only one of which would lead you back to Iasemión, but there was no way of knowing which. The traffic planner who had devised this horrible scheme must, in George's view, be either a schizophrenic or a devotee of Homer's *Odyssey* who had decided to replicate the ancient epic of homeless wandering in the streets of the capital city. The usual explanation, that the one-way system was designed to discourage the use of residential streets as through-routes, might have been correct but for the obvious fact that the streets *were* used as a through-route every morning and evening by a hard core of determined individuals, each one a modern Odysseus driving his powerful black Mercedes or BMW at high speed to and from the office. Speed bumps, pot-holes and badly parked cars did nothing to discourage them. Heroes in their own minds if in nobody else's, they were beating the system – the most enduring of all the pleasures of Greek life.

George had known the street of the jasmines since

childhood. A strange uncle had lived there in a fine old 1920s house with a neglected garden. A kind, brilliant, troubled man, a Professor of Physics at the Polytechnion, he suffered terrible bouts of depression. He had taken his own life in the 1980s, the house had been sold, demolished and replaced by a block of flats, its garden paved over with a car park. George could never pass the street without thinking of the old man, and the terrifying emptiness of his eyes the last time he had seen him.

He rang the bell at Number 12 and Olli appeared at the street door.

'The entryphone's broken,' she said. 'No one wants to spend the money to repair it.'

In the entrance hall of the apartment, under an enormous spotlit icon of St George and the dragon, blazing in gold and crimson, Olli introduced him to her parents. Courteous, pale, timid people in their sixties who, he could sense immediately, would struggle to survive in the cut-throat daily life of 21st-century Athens.

'I'm afraid Olli has brought you here in vain,' said her mother, with a quivering nervous energy that seemed capable of splitting marble. 'She thinks we need a burglar alarm.'

'Quite unnecessary,' said her father testily.

'Unfortunately,' said George, 'there are so many burglaries these days that...'

'Does an alarm deter them? I very much doubt it!'

'Of course it does,' said George. 'At least it makes the burglars think twice. They will always prefer an easy target.'

'So you say!'

'I'm only telling you what I know to be true,' said George. 'It's up to you if you choose to listen.'

'Let me show Mr Zafiris the apartment,' said Olli. 'It won't cost us anything to hear his advice.'

'It will cost us to follow it!' said her father.

'There's always a choice of security measures,' said George. 'Simple precautions cost nothing.'

'But you're in business, so you'll recommend whatever makes money for you.'

'That's not how I work.'

'It's how everyone works!'

'Don't be so rude to Mr Zafiris, father! He is Pandelís' uncle. I'm sure he'll give us impartial advice.'

'Family are the worst of all,' Olli's father went on, shaking his head fussily. 'They always think you're a soft touch. Well I'm telling you, Mr Zafiris, I am *not* a soft touch!'

'Let the man do his job,' said the mother. 'He's taken the trouble to…'

'I will decide, woman!' snapped the father. He turned to George. 'Since you're here, you may as well have a look and make your recommendations. Bear in mind that I'm in business too, I shall get other quotations, and I have a good mind not to install any security equipment at all! Olli, please show the gentleman the apartment.'

Coldly, Olli replied, 'Thank you father… Mr Zafiris, I'll show you where the burglars got in.'

She led him along a corridor decorated in faded 1970s style with hessian on the walls and bulky spotlights hanging from the ceiling. Opening a door at the far end she announced, 'There! The green bathroom!'

George saw that the window had been forced, its aluminium frame bent and the locking mechanism snapped off. Black smears of fingerprint dust were still scattered around the frame, as if devils had been playing there. He slid the window open.

'Can I get out there, onto the balcony?'

'Through the bedroom.'

She opened the adjoining door into a spectacular mess of a room, with clothes flung about in every direction. 'Ignore the chaos,' she said. 'The balcony is over there.'

He picked a path through an avalanche of shoes and magazines to the glazed door, peering out along the narrow balcony. A set of aluminium bars rested against the wall below the bathroom window. Above them the plaster around the embrasure was hacked away in four places and the marble sill smashed. At the other end of the balcony he noticed a rack hung with black lace underwear drying in the winter sun. Beyond it, practically touching the end of the balcony, the red metal roof of a storage shed.

'That's an easy way in,' he said.

Olli nodded.

'Did they leave from here too?'

'No. They used the door on the next balcony, over there.'

George checked the drop to the garden. Two to three metres. Easy with a ladder – or circus training.

'Did they hit all the rooms?'

'No. This one (mine) and my parents' bedroom. They had a quick scrabble through the *saloni,* but ignored the antiques, which are valuable. They must have been after jewellery and cash.'

He followed her round the rest of the apartment, checking all the possible entry points.

'The place is an open invitation to thieves,' he said.

'I know. Make your recommendations to my father. He's in a filthy mood today, but he'll calm down.'

'I've dealt with worse. Do they have any staff here?'

'A cleaning lady from Albania.'

'Trusted?'

'She's been with us for 20 years.'

'Did she see your necklace?'

'I don't know. You suspect her?'

'Just asking.'

'She doesn't usually clean inside cupboards. And anyway, why would she bother breaking in when she could just help herself?'

'To divert suspicion.'

'She's not the type.'

'There isn't a type.'

'You know what I mean. She's honest. A saint practically.'

'Does she have a husband? A brother?'

'A husband once upon a time. But he was a layabout and a drunkard, so she threw him out. I've never heard of any brothers.'

'Do you know any more about the acrobats?'

She eased a phone out of the tight back pocket of her trousers.

'Flamur and Fisnik Zamir.'

'Who gave you their names?'

'The man in the shop.'

'OK, I'd better talk to your parents.'

'And tell them what?'

'The obvious thing. They need better locks, an alarm system with laser beams, infra-red sensors, a secure telephone line to the police: the lot.'

'Don't overdo it!'

'You have to deliver a package these days.'

'They won't want it.'

'Of course. Especially at the price I quote.'

11

'The Flying Zamirs!' Colonel Sotiriou relished the words. 'I remember them well.'

'You've heard of therm?'

'Not only *heard*. I've seen them perform.'

'I don't think of you as a man who goes to the circus.'

'I have grandchildren, Mr Zafiris, and we all love the circus. The Zamir Twins wore bright blue tights and scarlet vests adorned with golden stars. They had thick curly black hair, magnificent muscles and the agility of monkeys. Juggling, balancing, leaping, somersaulting – they did it all. I'm sorry to hear they've turned to crime.'

'The crime is only an allegation.'

'Of course! It may turn out to be gossip. You must judge for yourself when you talk to them.'

'How can I do that?'

'I have their address.' He rattled it out, adding a phone number.

'Will they see me?'

'That depends on your skill in presenting yourself. Judging by the frequency with which you appear in my life, uninvited, you'll have no trouble… If I were you,' the Colonel added, 'I would appeal to their self-interest.'

'Valuable advice. I'll work on it.'

He was walking out through the doors of the police headquarters when his phone rang. An excited Olli was on the other end.

'I don't know how you did it,' she said, 'but my mother and father were completely convinced by your sales talk. Now they want a price.'

'That's a waste of time.'

'They've been discussing it earnestly for the past half hour. Father's had a change of heart, says he's been a fool. He's speaking of "in-depth structural reforms". Sounds like an official from the IMF.'

'Or a man in a mid-life crisis.'

'Whatever. You've talked them into it.'

'That's mad. I don't even know where to buy the stuff!'

'Better start your research.'

George swore to himself. Olli's parents must be even weirder than they appeared. Indecisive. Volatile. Hostile one moment, friendly the next. And now they wanted security equipment.

Needing help with this, he thought of Haris. Haris ran an electrical shop and loved gadgets. He always had ideas.

'I'll get you a quote,' said George. 'I've just thought of the perfect man for the job.'

Walking along Alexandras Avenue, he considered the matter of the Flying Zamirs. Colonel Sotiriou had advised appealing to their self-interest. It was either that or threatening them – greed or fear, unlikely to be anything in between. Given the lack of evidence, and their tough, itinerant profession, he didn't think much of his chances of threatening. Or of making the threats stick. They could always threaten back, probably with more power to hurt.

He dialled their number. A woman answered curtly, 'Balkan Transport Company.'

'I'd like to speak to Mr Zamir please.'

'Which one?'

'I don't mind. Whoever makes the decisions.'

'Who are you? What do you want?'

'My name is Zafiris. I'm a private investigator. I have a proposal for Mr Zamir. A very attractive proposal.'

'Hold on.'

George waited. At last a man's voice, thick with suspicion, growled: 'Zamir speaking. Who's that?'

George repeated his story.

'What sort of proposal?'

'You could call it an exchange.'

'Tell me.'

'10,000 euros for a diamond necklace.'

'I don't want a diamond necklace.'

'But I do. A special one, stolen from a house in Psyhikó last Saturday.'

'I know nothing about that.'

'The reward is 10,000. If you can help me find it, the money is yours.'

'Why do you offer this to me?'

'I was given your name.'

'By whom?'

'Someone who knows.'

'Are you a policeman?'

'No.'

'Who are you?'

'I'm an investigator, working for the owner of the necklace.'

'Your name again?'

'Zafiris.'

'That means nothing to me. I run a transport company.'

'The police have evidence linking you and your brother to the theft of that necklace. And many other stolen items.'

'Go to hell.'

George sat back in his chair and took a sip of beer. It was the reaction he had expected.

12

Haris was happy to be called. The shop was like a morgue, he said, and he might as well be a corpse himself for all the work he was getting. George sympathised, and they compared misery tales. Then George broke the news. He described the situation at Olli's house and the security measures it would need. Webcams, alarms, floodlights, lasers, infra-red movement sensors…

'They want all that?'

'Everything. They're nervous people. Recently burgled.'

'Fair enough.'

'You can supply it all, and fit it?'

'No problem. Obviously I need to see the place.'

'Ah,' said George. 'That you cannot do.'

'How can I give a quote?'

'Find a way.'

'But you're tying my hands!'

'They think I'm the contractor. It's too late to pull out now.'

George described the house, making rough guesses at the measurements. Haris wrote them down under protest. George said, 'If you want the work, give me a quote. If not, I'll turn the job down.'

'OK,' said Haris. 'You'll have it in an hour.'

'Thanks,' said George. 'One more thing. Your cousin the used car dealer.'

'What about him?'

'I need a price for a red Alfa Romeo Spider convertible, 1982, perfect condition. 90,000 kilometres on the clock.'

'No, George, don't tell me you're selling!'

'Hard times.'

'If I had the cash, I'd buy it today.'

'Ask him, will you?'

'Oh man, that hurts!'

'Tell me about it!'

George hung up. That was a good turn done, even if he'd never intended it.

Zoe came in, her mood unusually gentle. 'I've cooked rabbit with green olives,' she said. 'Are you hungry?'

'Extremely.'

Later that night, with a hot supper and half a bottle of Tselepos Merlot inside him, George enjoyed a rare hour of contentment. He and Zoe cleared up the kitchen while listening to a piano recital on the radio. He stretched out on the sofa and watched a documentary about code-breaking in the Second World War. Things were on the mend. Money trickling in, work on the horizon. He was a lucky man. Not everyone was so blessed...

Abruptly he remembered Wasim Khan. A pang of guilt raced through him. What had he done to find out more? Why had Wasim been attacked? What were the police doing about it? Sotiriou had said nothing more. The case would have the lowest priority. But if George took it on, who would pay him for his time? There was no incentive, no money at stake. The memory of Wasim, so vivid a few days ago, was already dimming in his mind.

Now that some cash was coming in, however, he felt he could spare a few hours. Drive over to Marathon, take another look around. It would be an excuse to drive the Alfa. If he was going to say goodbye to his beautiful car, he wanted to enjoy it to the maximum before the evil day arrived.

Next morning at ten he parked outside the seaside taverna, scene of the family lunch. He locked the car and crossed the road in the direction that Wasim had indicated, towards a clump of bushes on rising ground. On the skyline beyond stood a man with a dog. As George approached they waited, watching him all the way. The man wore khaki camouflage trousers, a black bomber jacket, baseball cap and dark glasses. A truncheon dangled from his belt.

'Good morning,' said George.

'What are you doing here?' was the only reply.

'Walking.'

'This is private land.'

'There are no fences, no signs.'

'I'm telling you.'

'Who's the owner?'

The man ignored the question. 'What do you want?'

'I wanted to see what's over the hill there.'

'Nothing.'

'There can't be nothing.'

'Fields. Vegetables. Nothing for you there.'

'I'm interested.'

'Why?'

'I knew someone who lived there.'

'No one lives there. If you want to walk, use the road.'

George stayed where he was. The man eyed him. With his blunt nose, pale lightless eyes and grizzled moustache, he was not particularly big or particularly fit, but he looked as if he could so some damage. The dog and the truncheon accentuated his menacing air.

'My friend was beaten up. He died from his injuries. That's where he lived.'

The man's face was blank.

'I hoped to find out something about him and the people he worked with.'

'There's no one there,' the man scowled.

'They work for you?'

'Who?'

'The Pakistanis.'

'I don't know any Pakistanis. Now get out of here before I lose my temper.'

'Are you in charge here?'

'I'm a guard.'

'Who's the boss?'

'None of your business. Off you go.'

'OK,' said George. He took a visiting card from his pocket. 'Think about it. If you saw anything, or have any information to give me, there's my number.'

'What is this? Are you a cop?'

'Private investigator. It says it on the card.'

'Why are you getting mixed up in this?'

'That's my business.'

He turned and walked back to the car.

From a café in Nea Makri, George phoned Colonel Sotiriou.

'I have no time!' shouted the Colonel by way of greeting.

'You never have time,' said George.

'A lawyer's been shot. A big name, so everyone's jumping.'

'Isn't it amazing how the system wakes up when it has to?'

'That *is* the system, Zafiris! Not amazing at all. What do you want?'

'I want you to give the Flying Zamirs a bit of a fright.'

'No way.'

'I don't expect you to do it personally. A junior officer will do nicely. One of the hundreds who sit around in police stations all over the country drinking coffee and comparing messages on their phones.'

'Leave out the cheap remarks! Those are my colleagues.'

'Pardon me. I just want one of these devoted public servants to pay the Zamirs a visit. They say they run a transport business. Really? What kind? Is it legitimate? Where are their trucks? Their depot? Company papers? Do they pay tax? And so on.'

Sotiriou said nothing.

'Colonel?'

'Hold on. News coming through… You were saying?'

George repeated his request wearily.

'It's not my department,' Sotiriou replied.

'I know that, Colonel!'

'So you're asking for another favour!'

'I am.'

'While I have a major political storm breaking over

my head!'

'I'm sorry, but…'

'Do you know who that lawyer was?'

'I don't,' said George.

'Pavlos Lazaridis. Does that mean anything to you?'

'Nothing.'

'That's how clever he was. And discreet… He represented politicians, shipowners, media people, everyone you've ever heard of. And when I'm talking…'

'Which politicians?'

'The old dynasties. Papandreou, Mitsotakis, Karamanlis, together with their families, lieutenants, retainers, and *compagnia bella*.'

'Any idea why he was shot?'

'That's what I am trying to work on while you waste my time with circus acrobats! Have a sense of proportion, Zafiris! Deal with this yourself!'

'It's a small favour.'

'Not this time! Try me next year.'

13

The news on the radio was all about the assassination of Lazaridis. Two men had made an appointment, entered his office, shot him dead at his desk and hurried out of the building, escaping by motorbike. The facts were minimal, the speculation immense. Experts, journalists and conspiracy theorists offered their explanations on television and radio. It must clearly be the work of terrorists. Or of anarchists, criminals, personal enemies, the mafia. Or perhaps one of those international societies – Bilderberg, the Freemasons, the New World Order, the Illuminati, Opus Dei, or unnamed dark forces of capitalism – against whose codes he must surely have offended...

Back in Athens, George drove the Alfa to the garage on Ippokratous Street, handed in the keys, and started to walk the short distance home.

On the way he became uncomfortably aware of a large car slowing down by his left shoulder: a black BMW X5 with tinted windows, its engine softly growling. The rear window slid down and a voice inside said, 'Get in.'

'Who's inviting me?' asked George.

'Zamir.'

'How did you find me?'

'Never mind. Just get in.'

George slipped his right hand into his jacket pocket and felt the cold metal of his Beretta.

'I don't get into strangers' cars,' he said.

'Don't piss around, buster. You want to talk, get in!'

'I have a better idea,' said George. 'There's a café up ahead. The Agamemnon. Meet me there.'

'You don't like my car?'

'The car's fine. It's the manners I dislike.'

'OK, see you at the *kafeneion*.'

The window slid shut and the car surged forward. Outside the café, its hazard lights flashing, a rear door opened and a short, muscular man stepped lightly onto the pavement, casting a wary look around.

'Mr Zamir?' said George.

The man's head turned to show a rugged face with glittering eyes and a sharp goatee beard. The hair hung in glistening black ringlets over his forehead, ears and collar. Alligator shoes, skin-tight burgundy trousers, a purple shirt and green leather blouson shimmered through a cloud of powerful and expensive scent. He was part gangster, part rock star.

'Flamur Zamir,' said the man, offering his hand.

'George Za –' he felt the bones crunch in his hand. He drew breath, managed to get 'Zafiris' out, and added, 'Thanks for stopping by.'

'It's my very great pleasure.'

'You'd better not leave the car there.'

Zamir turned and banged on the roof of the car twice. It slipped away.

'Shall we go in?' said Zamir.

'Why not?'

Zamir continued to glance around as he walked in, as if the place might be booby-trapped. He took in the café's yellowing walls, the old marble tables and rush-seated chairs, with a mixture of curiosity and distaste. He chose a table, the one George usually occupied, and sat down.

'What will you have?' said George.

'A Kaiser.'

George signalled to Dimitri, who was standing by suspiciously.

'One Kaiser, one Fix please.'

Zamir waited for Dimitri to remove himself, then got straight down to business.

'How serious is the reward that you spoke of?'

'Extremely serious.'

'Conditions?'

George thought quickly. 'The necklace has sentimental value. It must be the original, whole and undamaged.'

'Handover?'

'Any way you like.'

Zamir pursed his lips. 'This has to be extremely discreet. I want no connection to me, my family, or my business. I need a firewall. Guaranteed.'

'What kind of firewall?'

Zamir flared up. 'Whatever is necessary! You do not give my name to anyone. No emails, text messages, phone calls, no physical or electronic traces. Understood?'

'Of course.'

'You can give me this guarantee?'

'I believe I can.'

'Believe? That's not good enough.'

'OK, I can then.'

'That's better. Another thing: how did you get my name?'

'It was all over the neighbourhood.'

'What do you mean?'

'I asked people in Palió Psyhikó, and they all said it was you and your brother.'

Zamir's eyes registered this uneasily. The beer arrived.

'Yiamas!' said George.

'Yiamas!'

'My friend in the police remembers your circus shows.'

Zamir nodded. 'We are famous. All over the Balkans, Russia, Germany, Italy. *I Fratelli Volanti Zamir!*'

'I would have thought you had made enough money to retire.'

Zamir grimaced. 'Not so easy. I have a family, responsibilities…'

'Ex-wives?'

'No, thank God. Tell me, Zafiris, how soon can you get the cash?'

'How soon can you get the necklace?'

'As soon as you like.'

'Tomorrow?'

'Even today.'

'You have it in the car?'

Zamir tapped his breast pocket.

'You don't mess around,' said George.

The Albanian tilted his head in acknowledgement.

George said, 'I'll find out when my client can get the cash.'

He could not resist adding, 'They've just been burgled, so they may be short.'

Zamir pretended not to hear this remark. He took a long draught of beer as George found Olli's number.

Olli was at once excited, gushing with thanks, wanting to know every detail. He had difficulty bringing her attention to bear on his question.

'I have 3,000 euros of yours already. When can you get me another seven?'

'You have five!' she said. 'Not three.'

'Two is my fee.'

'Two thousand? How long have you spent on this?'

'Plenty of time. And it's not over yet. We have to see it through to the end.'

'Oh,' she said. 'I didn't realise it would be so expensive. Seven thousand! That will take a few days.'

'Get onto it right away.'

Ending the call, he turned to Zamir.

'About a week,' he said.

'Fine,' said Zamir. 'A package containing the necklace will be exchanged for the money in a safe place which I will indicate to you by a telephone call. If you are followed, or play any trick, any trick at all – and I know every single one of them – the deal's off. And *you* will go straight onto my trouble list.'

'What's the trouble list?'

'A bad place where you don't want to go.'

'I don't plan to.'

Zamir nodded understandingly and took another sip of beer. Suddenly he had a business card in his hand, produced so rapidly that George blinked in disbelief.

'Flamur Zamir, Chief Executive, Balkan Transport Company' was printed on one side, with an address in Asprópyrgos on the reverse. That at least seemed authentic.

'How many vehicles do you have?' asked George.

'Twelve trucks, four sprinters. Why? You need something moved?'

'No. Just curious.'

'And you?'

'Just one vehicle.'

'Ha ha. I didn't mean how many vehicles! Are you ex-police?'

'No. Ex-bank.'

'Bank? Smart! Very, very smart!'

'What do you mean?'

Zamir shook his head. 'That is so beautiful. You know all the rich clients, you offer protection…'

'Only in a general way.'

'Oh yes!' Zamir was smiling happily at the thought. 'Only general! Ha ha! I like your style. You and me can make a very nice business.'

'I doubt it.'

'Oh yes! You offer security to your clients. They accept? It's a nice deal. They refuse? Oh dear, burglary! Oh dear, car stolen!'

'That's known as a protection racket.'

'No.' Zamir beckoned him closer, into his cloud of scent. 'You do nothing criminal. Leave that to your friends. You know nothing about this.'

George said, 'Don't be a fool, Zamir. The police – even the Greek police – would figure that out very fast.'

'I know people who do this. They make plenty of money.'

'And then go to prison. No thanks.'

'They are not in prison. They are free. Living in big houses.'

George began to lose patience. 'Maybe they're free, maybe they're not. It doesn't matter. The point is, it's illegal and unethical.'

Zamir laughed pleasantly. 'You are a very funny man.'

'I'm not trying to be funny. I hope you are.'

'Not at all! It's a serious business proposal!'

'It stinks.'

'I leave it with you.'

'The answer is no.'

Again Zamir laughed.

George stood up. 'I have to go,' he said.

Zamir glanced down at his unfinished beer. 'We are still drinking,' he said.

'I'm not thirsty any more.'

Displeased, Zamir stood up too. 'I will not drink alone,' he said. 'Don't forget, Mr Zafiris.'

'Forget what?'

'What we said.'

'I'll remember the good things.'

'Always the good things!' said Zamir He waved Dimitri over, put ten euros in his hand, and grandly refused the change.

14

Despite the 'capital controls', which limited bank withdrawals to 420 euros per week, Olli produced the cash within 24 hours. George telephoned Zamir and was given directions to a country club on the road to Varibobi, where Olli was to appear in a taxi, alone, at eleven-thirty that night. George passed on the instructions to Olli. The cash was to be in an envelope, unsealed on the seat beside her. No one was to follow her or be told where she was going.

'That's impossible,' she objected. 'My parents will ask. So will Pandelís.'

'Make up a story.'

'I don't like it.'

'It will be all right.'

'Why don't I send someone else? They don't know me.'

'Don't be so sure. You have a Facebook page?'

'Of course.'

'Then they know you.'

'Why does it have to be me?'

'You may also want to be sure it's your necklace.'

'I'd prefer it if you came with me.'

'I can't.'

'Why not?'

'They said no. Explicitly.'

'You asked them?'

'Of course. First thing.'

'What are they afraid of?'

'A trick.'

'Then let's give them one. You can be the driver.'

'I don't have a taxi.'

'I'll get one. Meet me outside the old Bluebell Café in Psyhikó at ten-thirty.'

'Olli, they said no.'

'You asked if you could drive the taxi?'

'I asked if I could accompany you.'

'That's different. Don't worry. It will be dark. Wear a cap if you're worried.'

'This isn't a game.'

'I know. That's why I want you there. I'm scared.'

He thought about it. It wasn't such a bad idea.

'I'll come,' he said.

At ten-thirty he parked his Alfa in the square and walked over to the kiosk in its metallic glare of neon-lit refrigerators, magazines and shiny packets of snacks. It was a cold evening, with rain in the air. A yellow taxi was parked at the kerb a few metres to the right of the kiosk. No driver, one passenger in the back. His phone rang.

'It's me,' she said. 'The keys are in the ignition.'

George opened the driver's door, saw her shadowy face give him a nervy smile, and got in.

'What did you tell your parents?' he asked. 'And Pandelís?'

'Girls' night out. Don't worry, driver! Let's go and get this horrible business over.'

As they drove through Kifissia the skies opened with a mighty crack of thunder and a sudden onslaught of rain. The shining streets were immediately clogged with honking traffic and hurrying pedestrians. The rain brought memories of those same streets five years ago, when he had raced to save his friend Hector Pezas from a death-trap at a politician's mansion. He had arrived too late. Hector tried to shoot his way out, stopped four men, but was hit himself. George nearly lost his mind over that, the guilt stabbing at him mercilessly even as he told himself that Hector had gone into the situation against George's advice. To help a lady. As George was doing now.

He had told Zoe this evening that he was out on a job. She had asked no details, only said, 'Be careful. I don't like it when you work at night.'

'It's fine,' he said. 'Routine stuff.'

But it was not routine, and a sense of foreboding kept him uneasy all along the road.

He pulled up at the Florida Estate country club, in a well-lit car park watched over by a guard in a little white hut. He turned the car to face the road, switched off the engine and listened to the clattering of rain on the roof of the taxi. The clock on the dashboard read eleven-fifteen.

'Whose is the car?' he asked.

'Belongs to a friend.'

'Must be a good friend.'

'He is.'

'I've never heard of anyone lending a taxi.'

She did not reply.

'You're not saying much. Are you OK?'

'Not really.'

'Just stay calm.'

'I'm not a calm person.'

'Then breathe deeply, and listen to your breathing.'

'If I could hear it above the rain…'

'Try,' he said. 'It will help.'

They sat without speaking for a few minutes. Off to the right a single headlamp beam began drilling along the tree-lined road towards them. As it approached, it slowed and angled in to the car park, swinging across them and lighting the interior of the cab. In the rear-view mirror George saw Olli's face, pale and tense in the icy glare.

'Here's our man,' said George. 'Money ready?'

'Yes.'

'Don't let go of it until you have the necklace in your hand and you're sure it's the right one.'

Olli tried to say something but the sound stuck in her throat.

A big German motorbike drew up next to the taxi. Its rider, in full leathers and helmet, raised himself from the handlebars and sat upright.

'Lower your window,' said George.

As she did so, a gauntleted hand reached in.

'Where's the necklace?' asked Olli in a strangled voice, barely audible against the drumming of the rain.

'Louder!' said George.

She asked again, raising her voice, and the gauntlet withdrew. It returned with a slim black box.

'Shall I give him the money?' asked Olli, bewildered.

'Check the box.'

She reached for it, but as her hand moved another headlamp beam appeared, followed swiftly by two more, turning into the car park. All three stopped, blocking the exit. The gauntleted hand drew back as if it had been scorched. The bike leapt away and vanished between the car headlights. At once one of the cars began manoeuvring to turn round and give chase, but it lost precious seconds and by the time it was on the road the motorbike's lights were already far off into the night.

'What's happened?' asked Olli.

'Let's see.'

Two black figures were approaching, picking their way through the puddles.

George knew who they were, and what they would say.

'Car papers, identity card, driving licence.'

George wearily handed over his ID and licence before reaching for the glove compartment where he hoped the taxi driver kept all his documents. His fingers found a plastic folder among some magazines. The policeman took the documents and walked back to his car, leaving his colleague standing in the rain.

'How the hell did they get here?' asked Olli.

'How do you think?'

'I can't imagine. It's an incredible coincidence.'

'Bullshit. Someone tipped them off, and it wasn't me.'

'And it wasn't me!' cried Olli indignantly.

'Then you must have told someone who did.'

'No, I swear.'

'Swear all you like. You can forget your necklace. The

Zamirs won't give you a second chance.'

'I didn't tell anyone!'

'Who knew about this, apart from you and me?'

'No one.'

'Someone must have done. The police don't go around in packs of three patrol cars just to check people's papers. Certainly not on a rainy night!'

The policeman was back. George lowered his window, the rain spitting in.

'This is not your taxi,' said the policeman.

'That's right. I'm borrowing it.'

'Your licence is not a taxi driver's licence.'

'I'm using the car privately.'

'You have a passenger.'

'She's not a passenger, she's a friend.'

'What's her name?'

'Olli Papaspirou.'

The policeman stood in silence, the rainwater spilling off his shoulders and arms and splashing in through the window.

'I could book you for driving a taxi without a suitable licence.'

'I hope you won't,' said George.

'Who was the man on the bike?'

'He wanted to sell us something.'

'What?'

'A necklace.'

'This is a strange place to buy a necklace.'

'Yeah.'

'Did you buy it?'

'No.'

'Why not?'

'Because you arrived.'

'Why did he clear off like that?'

'I don't know.'

'You don't know?'

The policeman took a torch from his pocket, shone it slowly around the inside of the cab. George prayed that Olli had had the sense to hide the money.

'What's that?'

'Just an envelope.'

'Let me see.'

She handed it over with a groan.

The policeman opened the envelope and flicked through the notes.

'This is a lot of money to carry around.'

'Not if you're buying a necklace,' said Olli.

'What is this necklace?'

'It's what my friend said!'

'You had a rendezvous?'

'Of course!'

'What is the name of the person who agreed to sell it to you?'

Olli became confused. 'You want his name?'

'And his address or phone number.'

She squeezed George's shoulder. 'Do you have his details?'

George was relieved when she stopped talking. Every word she spoke took her further from seeing her necklace again.

'I'll give you a number,' said George, 'and a name.'

'Go ahead.'

'The name is Sotiriou. Constantine Sotiriou.'

The policeman tapped the name into his phone. 'Number?'

'You can find that in the police directory. He's head of the Violent Crimes Unit.'

'Don't try to be funny.'

'I'm not. Call him. Speak to him.'

The policeman looked lost. 'He's selling a necklace?'

'No,' said George. 'I'm on a job, working for him. We had a plan, and I am talking about a precise plan, fully worked out, with timings and everything. It was all going fine until you turned up. So I want to know who sent you, and with such impeccable timing.'

'That's operational information.'

'Sure! That's how you screw up, cover up, and never learn a single lesson.'

'Give me your phone number,' said the policeman. 'I'm going to check your story.'

15

On the road home, George's phone rang. A coldly furious Flamur Zamir told him he did not like being betrayed.

'I said no tricks, and you pull two. First, you drive the taxi. Next, you call the police! What's your game, Zafiris? Do you want the necklace or not?'

'The girl was scared, so I came along to protect her. I don't know who told the police. The girl denies it. She wants the necklace, so she's not going to mess things up, is she?'

'Normally you are dead, Zafiris.'

'Don't blame me.'

'I blame you!'

'You're making a mistake. The police…'

'Who told the police? What bastard made a deal with me, a deal with the police also, then he can collect from both sides? Big smart-ass bastard! The mistake is yours!'

'Hold on to the necklace,' said George. 'We'll try again.'

'How can we try again? I want to do business with you, but now I don't trust you.'

'Let me give you a roadmap.'

'I don't want a fucking roadmap! I want the reward! End of story! Who wants a roadmap?'

'I'm going to find out who told the police. Then we'll make a new rendezvous, more secure – just you and me, no girl – and the exchange will go ahead.'

'You do that.'

Zamir ended the call.

'You heard?' said George.

'He doesn't sound happy.'

'Damn right.'

'*Normally you are dead.* What did he mean?'

'That's the punishment for betrayal.'

'Oh God, I don't like this!'

'You shouldn't have told the police.'

'I didn't!'

'There's no way they could have turned up without a tip-off. It had to come from you, either directly or through careless talk.'

'Mr Zafiris, you're wrong. I was very, very careful.'

'Not careful enough. Someone heard you talking.'

'But I didn't talk about it!'

'We'll see.'

'What do you mean?'

'I'll talk to the police, find out who informed them.'

'You can do that?'

'I most certainly can.'

She remained defiant. 'I'd be very interested to know.'

16

The next day George drove to the airport to collect Nick. Zoe had persuaded him to fly in from Newcastle for an interview with his uncle Stelios. There was no real prospect of a job, and George suspected that both Nick and Stelios were going through the motions in order to pacify the matriarchs, Zoe and Maria. This annoyed George intensely. He was always happy to see his son, but this visit was futile. Another six hundred euros would go up in kerosene smoke and everybody was supposed to feel happy.

George met his son in the crowded arrivals hall and they hugged each other joyfully. Nick looked fit and happy, while George was aware of looking out of shape and somewhat depressed. They picked up the Alfa from the car park and drove towards Athens on the Attiki Odos, skirting the foothills of Mount Penteli. Nick reacted excitedly to the sight of his native land, the snow-tipped mountains etched in razor-sharp light, dissolving in the distance to a silvery blue mist. 'I never realise how much I miss this,' said Nick. 'It's like opening a window on the first morning of spring. Suddenly winter's over.'

'And then you get used to it,' said George. 'It even begins

to oppress you.'

'Hey come on, pops, don't be a misery guts!'

'OK, cancel that. It's lovely. Fills your heart with optimism, I admit that. On certain days you feel you're superhuman, breathing the air of the gods. Then the reality hits you – a sickening lurch in the guts.'

'Ah. Nothing's changed, then.'

'Let me correct that. The past six months something has definitely altered, hard to say just what. Spirits have lightened. It's not that our problems have gone away – far from it – but now we're used to dealing with them. The worst was the first seven years, when we all remembered how good it was before. Now we've forgotten that, we're hardened by austerity. We know how to deal with it.'

'That's progress of a kind.'

'Sure.'

'You know we hear nothing about Greece in the English news? As if it no longer exists. They used to love showing the riots in Athens. Molotov cocktails, anarchists, burning cars! Now it's all Brexit and Trump, nothing else.'

'Sounds boring. How did either of those great nations fall for these simplistic ideas?'

'That's the big question, and everyone's asking it too late. The media can't work out how a democracy can produce such weird results. They rack their brains about it 24 hours a day, while the victors strut about saying "Get over it!"'

George laughed. 'In a way we're lucky. We have a totally useless government, a collection of incompetent fantasists, but we have an advantage over our northern neighbours: we don't expect any better.'

'Which is worse,' said Nick, 'Expecting good government and getting rubbish, or expecting rubbish and getting it?'

'At least the English live in hope,' said George. 'We lost that long ago.'

'But if your hopes are always dashed, why not accept despair? Make it your friend?'

They entered the city, the traffic slowing to a crawl on Liosion Street. The sight of a gypsy woman begging with her child seemed to trigger a thought for Nick.

'How's mother?' he asked.

'Painting again.'

'Hey, that's great.'

'Seems to be. For me as well as her.'

'How come?'

'She leaves me alone.'

'Is that what you want?'

'I can think of nothing better.'

George pulled into the garage on Ippokratous Street and handed over the keys to the man in the booth. Together they toiled up the car-clogged pavement of Aristotle Street, past the Café Agamemnon, where Dimitri waved and smiled as he continued wiping tables. George opened the plate-glass door to No 43, unleashing the lobby's strange smells of last month's cooking and floor wax, its shadowy vista of empty plant tubs and letter boxes, the shaft of dust-flecked light down the stair well.

'Suicide Hall!' said Nick. 'It's good to be back.'

George smirked. No one had killed himself in there, but a dark mood one day had given birth to that name, and it had stuck.

Zoe was waiting on the landing. She kissed her son with tears in her eyes, held him close and welcomed him home. It was moments like these that she loved best.

While Nick and Zoe exchanged news, George went into another room and called Haris. He wanted to check how things were going in the Papaspirou house.

Haris reported that all was well, while remarking *sotto voce* on the extreme oddness of the household.

'They're obviously rich,' said Haris, 'but they don't enjoy it. They're anxious the whole time.'

'About what?'

'Everything! Politics, immigration, family, money.'

'Help them, Haris! You're the security expert.'

Haris laughed. 'I'm not a psychiatrist! They're crazy.'

'The whole family?'

'Mainly the mother. She's working on everyone else. Slowly, a little every day.'

'Does she bother you?'

'She comes in and offers me coffee. I say yes, that would be lovely, and then she starts asking questions. What happens if a mouse sets off the alarm? Can you get electrocuted if you touch the equipment? Isn't it a fire hazard? Does the alarm attract thieves? Is it all right in the rain? What about thunderstorms? When will I finish? What day? Morning or afternoon? Can we have a clear calendar? She holds me up for twenty minutes, then wanders off and forgets the coffee.'

'Where's her husband?'

'Hiding in his study. Staring at share prices. From time to time she drops in on him and he yells at her to get out.'

'Have you met the son?'

'No.'

'Is he abroad?'

'No, he lives in Athens. He's never at home. I can't say I blame him. How that girl stands it I don't know.'

'And her boyfriend? Pandelís?'

'He's been here once or twice.'

'Doing what?'

'Hanging around, lusting after her.'

'Do you hear them talking?'

'No. Why?'

George explained about the tip-off to the police at the Florida Estate. 'If she didn't tell them,' he said, 'someone else did. Someone who knew what she was up to.'

'You think it's the boyfriend?'

'He's the obvious candidate.'

'Want me to talk to him?'

'Just keep your ears open.'

Haris was silent for a few moments.

'How open?' he asked with a change of tone.

'What do you mean?'

'I can add a little extra functionality to the system. Very simple. Totally invisible.'

'And unethical.'

'Borderline, I'd say.'

'It's not borderline, Haris, it's plain unethical. And illegal."

'Really?'

'Don't tempt me, Haris. I want to keep things clean.'

'OK.' Haris sighed. 'You're the boss.'

17

George meant what he said about keeping things clean. It was the way he liked to do things. Way back in his youth he had decided: no more intentions, no more empty promises, no tricks, no lies, no aces up the sleeve. Still, the thought of Haris' offer kept coming back to him over the next twenty-four hours. Twice it seriously tempted him. The first time was when his phone rang and Flamur Zamir, his voice spiked with anger, informed him that the price of the necklace had now risen to 20,000 euros. George tried to protest, but Zamir was adamant. 'Take it or leave it, Mr Zafiris. You have until 10 pm tomorrow.'

'They won't pay 20,000.'

'If they want it, they will.'

'That's not good business.'

'Don't tell me what's good business! You invite the police to the party, Mr Zafiris, you pay double.'

'I did not invite the police.'

'Someone did!'

'It wasn't me and it wasn't the girl. Don't push your luck on the price, Zamir.'

'No more discussion. You want it? The price is 20.'

The second time was when Nick returned from his job interview at the Katramis office. He had met Pandelís and they'd gone for a drink together. Pandelís told him all about the burglary and the botched meeting with Zamir. Nick was amused as he told the story, but George was astonished. He listened so quietly that Nick asked if he was feeling all right.

'I'm fine,' he said, 'but I need to go and call someone. Right now.'

'Go,' said Nick. 'See you later.'

George rang Olli at once.

'Your boyfriend knows about the stolen necklace, Olli. Not only that, but he knows about the reward, Zamir, the police – every last detail.'

'How do you know that?'

'How do I know? Because Pandelís told my son!'

'That's impossible!'

'Yeah right! The impossible thing happened! How the hell did Pandelís find out?'

'I've no idea.'

'Then you must be schizophrenic, or a sleep talker, because the only person who could *possibly* have told him is you.'

'I did *not* tell him! I have no *reason* to tell him. It would be crazy!'

'Listen, Olli, you wouldn't be the first woman on earth to do illogical things.'

'That's a sexist remark!'

'It's still true.'

'You think I'm so damn stupid I would tell my boyfriend the one thing I don't want him to know? If you think that, Mr Zafiris, you certainly don't understand women!'

'How do you explain it?'

'I can't.'

'Thanks a bunch!'

'I can't. I can't! What more can I say?'

'Who have you discussed this with?'

'Only you.'

'All right.' George attempted to calm himself down. 'Let's think about this. You and I have spoken in person and on the phone. When we spoke on the phone, was Pandelís with you?'

'No.'

'Could he have overheard?'

'Absolutely not.'

'Where was he?'

'Not with me.'

'Do you talk in your sleep?'

'What?'

'Seriously.'

Her tone changed. 'Mr Zafiris, I do not sleep with Pandelís.'

'Really?'

'I'm old-fashioned that way.'

'Surely, though…'

'Forget it! That is not his source of information!'

'Do you keep a diary? Or post on social media?'

'Diary no. Social media yes, but I have never mentioned the necklace or the burglary.'

George thought about this.

'Are you at home now?' he asked.

She said she was.

'Is Haris there?'

'Yes.'

'OK. Don't go out. I'll call back in a few minutes.'

When Haris answered his phone, George told him a story about his brother Hector. How he had once fitted a listening device in a politician's phone.

'I remember it well,' said Haris. 'I helped him.'

'Would you recognise one of those devices?'

'Of course.'

'Can you check Olli's phone, and see if it's got anything similar inside it?'

'I can, but it's unlikely.'

'Why?'

'It's all done with software now. Download it onto the target phone, it sits there invisibly and sends you all the goodies by email.'

'You can't trace it or disable it?'

'Trace it, no. Disable it, possibly. Depends on the software.'

'So how could we be sure if her phone was being spied on?'

'If you know who's doing it, and you can get to their phone, you can install spy software on that. Monitor their monitoring. Tit for tat.'

'That would prove it?'

'It would, but why do it? It's obvious that he's using some form of surveillance. It may not be on her phone. He could have planted a device in her room. These things aren't expensive, and they're getting easier to buy.'

'OK, so we could buy this software and ask Olli to install it on her boyfriend's phone?'

'We could. But how is that going to help you get the necklace back?'

'It might stop that idiot Pandelís going to the police again.'

116

'We can do that more easily another way. Just keep the sensitive information off Olli's phone. Talk to her face to face, making sure her phone is in another room.'

'Can you put her on?'

'Sure. I'll find her.'

George waited a minute or two, wondering what sort of person would feel justified in spying on his girlfriend like that. When Olli answered he told her his suspicions.

She said, 'That's impossible,' for the second time that afternoon.

'I know it's a shock,' said George, 'but it explains a lot.'

She cut in brusquely. 'I don't want to discuss this now!'

'You're going to have face this sooner or later, Olli. It's coercive behaviour and it's going to bring you great unhappiness.'

The phone went dead.

18

George found Nick and Zoe in the kitchen drinking coffee.

'Come and join us,' said Nick.

George sat down.

Nick described the scene at the Katramis office. At first only Pandelís and his father were there. They asked a few questions which Nick answered, all very calm and professional. Then Maria came in, short-tempered and impatient, and things began to fall apart. She showed no interest in Nick and kept changing the subject, switching the focus of the discussion onto her problems, answering her phone and holding loud conversations that prevented the proper business of the meeting. Eventually she said, 'I can't sit around here wasting any more time. I have to go to the Ministry.'

This reminded Stelios that he had phone calls to make. It was left to Pandelís to show Nick out.

'That's just bloody rude,' said George.

'It was kind of them to see you,' said Zoe.

'It would have been kinder if I'd had a chance to say anything.'

'That's typical of Maria,' said George. 'Totally self-obsessed.'

'You did what you had to do,' said Zoe. 'Showed your face. Turned up on time, polite, well-dressed. You did turn up on time I hope?'

'Fifteen minutes early.'

'Good! All that counts. More than you might think. If you show good manners in Greece, you stand out from the crowd.'

'I know,' said Nick, 'but still! I've flown all the way from Newcastle so they could interview me. Instead I listened to Maria's telephone conversations.'

'Never mind.'

'I think I ought to see them again.'

'Don't do that. They won't like it.'

'They don't know anything about me.'

'Did you give them your CV?'

'Of course.'

'That's enough. They'll do the rest. Mark my words.'

Nick glanced sceptically towards his father. George made an effort to reassure him. 'I'm sure your mother's right,' he said. 'These things work in mysterious ways.'

Nick frowned. 'Extremely mysterious.'

'Did you catch anything of Maria's phone conversations?' asked George.

'Only the whole damned lot.'

'What were they about?'

'George!' cried Zoe. 'That's none of your business.'

'She wasn't exactly private about it,' said Nick. 'It was all about some elaborate tax deal.'

'Of course,' said George.

'Why of course?'

'She's a tax inspector.'

119

Nick looked up in astonishment. 'A tax inspector? A public servant?'

'She's paid by the public. Whether she serves it or not is highly questionable.'

'So what's she doing at her husband's business?'

'Moonlighting, I expect. And making a great deal of money.'

'Is that legal?'

'Haha!'

'We shouldn't be discussing this,' said Zoe. 'She's a very capable woman. And she has a perfect right to visit her husband and son at their office.'

'Perhaps Nick needs to understand why she sabotaged the interview.'

'She did not sabotage the interview!' said Zoe. 'She's busy, that's all.'

'Busy,' said George, 'in that chaotic, narcissistic way that wastes everybody else's time. If that's being capable…'

'George, watch your tongue! Nick could be working for these people!'

'He needs to know what he's letting himself in for.'

'Your opinions are irrelevant.'

'OK,' said George. 'Let Nick decide for himself. He's had a taste of Maria's style. You think she's going to improve?'

'You have a way of judging everybody…'

'Nick judged her! You would too if you were honest, and not so blinded by family loyalty. She's a monster.'

'…who has been very kind to us!'

'She represents everything that's wrong with this country.'

'Oh come on!'

'What Greece needs is…'

'Don't start telling me…'

'…concrete proposals to get rid of the clientelistic system, and concrete measures to fight corruption.'

'Katramis can certainly supply the concrete,' said Nick.

'This is not about politics!' cried Zoe. 'It's about a job for Nick!'

'Hold on,' said Nick. 'Please don't argue. I can make up my own mind. Listen, Dad: if she's a tax inspector how much time is she going to spend at the family office? I probably wouldn't see her much – assuming they gave me a job at all…'

'Exactly,' said Zoe. 'Just forget about her. She's your aunt, so you must treat her with respect.'

'If you can,' said George.

'Leave it!' said Zoe bitterly. 'Give the boy a chance!'

'Happy to,' said George, raising his hands. 'By the way, did they say when they would let you know?'

'No. They just said "good to see you".'

'You flew 3000 kilometres for that?'

'George!' Zoe exploded. 'Will you leave it?'

He forced a smile. 'I'm leaving it,' he said. 'Let's hope it works out.'

He added, 'It would be lovely to have you back in Athens, Nick. We miss you.'

19

With just over 24 hours to go until the deadline, George decided to hustle Olli along. He called her and arranged to meet.

She was in a listless, alienated state. Asked what she planned to do about the necklace, she shrugged her shoulders. About Pandelís she merely said, 'What choice do I have?'

'Have you asked him why he bugged your phone?'

'No.'

'Don't you think you should? It is a crime after all.'

'Surely it's not a crime!'

'You don't think it's his right?'

She smirked. 'Perhaps he thinks it is.'

'It's not. There's legislation about this. Privacy. Confidentiality.'

'It doesn't matter.'

'I'm telling you it does. This is a form of abuse.'

'Forget it, Mr Zafiris. I'm more worried about the necklace.'

'Then you must act quickly. And find another 10,000 euros.'

'I don't know how I'm going to do that.'

'In that case you'll lose it.'

She said nothing.

'Are you happy to lose it? We have until ten tomorrow night.'

Olli gazed at him hopelessly. 'What do you do when you can't do anything?'

George gave her a compassionate look. 'You want my advice?'

'You bet I do!'

'The first rule is, don't give up. The second rule is – in my book at least – talk to a good friend. In my case it would be Haris. He always has an idea.'

'What, apart from sex?'

George was taken aback. 'Has he tried it on with you?'

'Of course.'

'That's extremely unprofessional of him.'

'Don't worry.'

'I do worry.'

'I couldn't care less. He's a man, isn't he?'

'Married as it happens. And doing a job for your parents. Who certainly didn't employ him to seduce their daughter!'

'Relax, Mr Zafiris. He hasn't "seduced" me.'

'No, but he's tried.'

'Big deal! A girl doesn't grow up in Greece without facing plenty of male lust. We learn to deal with it very young. If we don't, we're finished.'

'I'm still going to have a word with him.'

'Please don't. I would feel betrayed.'

'He needs to learn some professional standards.'

'Another time. Let's get on with the necklace, shall we?'

'Fine. Let's talk to Haris.'

They found him in the kitchen, trying to install an infra-red sensor while Olli's mother, cigarette in hand, told him a melancholy story about a childhood visit to a dying uncle in

New York. He was clearly in need of rescue.

George asked for a private word. Mrs Papaspirou crushed her cigarette in the ashtray with quivering fingers and fluttered elegantly out of the room.

'How are we going to get round this crook Zamir?' said George. 'He's doubled the price and Olli can't raise the cash. We need one of your brilliant ideas.'

'What's he like?' asked Haris.

George described him. 'Squat, muscular, cunning. Oily-haired, loudly dressed. Typical circus acrobat, I suspect.'

'An acrobat?' Intrigued, Haris stopped what he was doing.

'That's right. Once famous. Now retired.'

'How old?'

'Forty-five? Fifty max.'

'Still got the old fire in his belly?'

'I'd say so.'

'He must be furious with you.'

'He is.'

'He trusted you. You let him down. Do that twenty metres up in a circus tent and you're dead.'

'I understand that.'

'Perhaps you don't.'

'No one likes to be let down.'

'It's more than that. I understand because I was a diver. We had to rely on people one hundred percent. Loyalty or death. No lapses or mistakes.'

'Fair enough.'

'You're a problem to him. He doesn't trust you, and never will.'

'I just want that necklace back.'

'OK,' said Haris sitting back on his heels. 'You want me to deal with him?'

'Will he trust *you*?'

'I know what to say.'

'Can you get the price down?'

'I'll have a damn good try.'

George left the house and walked down through the tree-lined streets of Psyhikó to Leoforos Kifissias, where he picked up a bus for the centre of town. The seats were packed with Ukrainian and Albanian women: carers, cooks and cleaners returning home from work. Craggy-faced, overweight, with slow, blank, weary eyes. He thought of Wasim Khan and all the other outsiders from even poorer countries, allowed to live in Greece and work for wretched wages.

An old man stood up to get off the bus, leaving a folded newspaper on his seat. George sat down and glanced at the paper, which was open at an opinion piece about the Greek crisis. 'Despite these bitter years of austerity we are still without a roadmap to dramatically downsize the public sector.' True enough, thought George, and Maria Katramis would be a great place to start. 'We need to see the exact number of civil servants that won't be replaced...' Right again! Do it by natural wastage. 'To transform the public banks into a healthy private financial sector...' That was wishful thinking, but it would certainly help... 'To open the markets and jobs currently closed for too many young people...' That would transform the country and bring new hope to every family in the land...

His phone rang. A harsh voice crackled in his ear.

'Zafiris? This is Sotiriou. I need your help. Can you come to my office?'

'I can.'

'When?'

'In twenty minutes.'

'Perfect.'

George wondered what this was about. He closed his eyes and let himself be carried along in the rattling, thudding, wheezing box of voices and tired limbs, south towards the centre of Athens.

20

Colonel Sotiriou was in one of his more manic moods, his bald head shining with an eerie radiance as he flung out ideas in a rapid, scintillating rush. Half hidden by the stacks of paper on his desk, his hands hacked the air as he spoke. His discourse was large and not entirely under control. It took in the whole of Greek history from the Bronze Age to the present – a story, as he put it, of 'grandeur and stupidity absurdly combined'.

'We invented democracy but we are the last on earth to have it. We have a *plutocracy* instead. Government by the rich. A dictatorship of money. We need to change this! We need to end the privileges of the shipowners, the military, the Orthodox Church...'

George tried to object. 'We have a socialist government.'

'Ha! Socialist! In name perhaps, but they are plutocrats, every one of them.'

'Forgive me, Colonel, but is this the reason you asked to see me?'

'I'm building up to that! Let me give you the context.'

'I've got the context nice and clear. Just tell me where this is leading.'

'It's leading to national suicide.'

'I take that as read,' said George.

'You must never do that! We need to act. You, me, anyone with a conscience. We have to stop complaining and *take action!*'

'How? Where? When?'

'We begin in our own lives. By refusing to compromise our standards of integrity.'

'Agreed. Totally impractical, but agreed.'

'Think of Mahatma Gandhi. Martin Luther King. Passive resistance was their way. Non-violence. Healing the sick nation. The *insane* nation!'

'That's an enormous task.'

'Of course. There must be no delay.'

George was becoming exasperated. 'All right, Colonel, I'll grant you all that. Now please tell me why you called me in and what you want me to do!'

The Colonel's eyebrows shot up. 'Do? Well now, there's an offer!'

George waited. 'So?'

As if he had run out of fuel, the Colonel slowed down dramatically. His eyes glowing dully, he muttered, 'I've told you before, Zafiris, there is an informal alliance of like-minded people. Trying, in an unsystematic way, to reform the country.'

'I remember.'

'Good! So: following this latest outrage it's time to organise.'

'What outrage?'

Sotiriou heaved a sigh. 'My lawyer friend, Pavlos Lazaridis, was killed last week. That was bad enough. But now the Minister of Justice has announced that the Lazaridis office is sealed until further notice, preventing all investigation of the crime. No one can enter unless personally authorised by the Minister.'

'With what justification?'

'You may well ask! The official reason is that "reactionary political interests are implicated", and the Ministry wishes to ensure complete "independence" in the investigation. So no police! Only Ministry apparatchiks who will scour the office for compromising documents, clear them out, and only then allow us in!'

'That stinks.'

'To put it mildly. We must stop it.'

'How do you propose to do that?'

'With your help, Zafiris.'

George was wary. 'I hope this isn't one of your suicide missions.'

'Not at all.'

'Tell me.'

Sotiriou flashed one of his most sinister smiles. 'We need to get into that office!'

'That's going to be difficult.'

'Of course.'

'And dangerous.'

'There are risks, but we will minimise them.'

'Do you have a plan of some kind?'

'I'm relying on you for the details.'

'Where is the office?'

'Amerikis 23. Bang in the centre.'

'A big building?'

'You need to take a look. I thought of you, Zafiris, not so

much for your own talents – which I respect of course – as that of your assistant, Mr Pezas. He was a navy frogman, I believe?'

'Is the office under water?'

'Don't be facetious. He's a man of method.'

'You want him to break in?'

'Break, slide, slip in – I don't mind! You may leave the precise method of entry to the other members of your team.'

'There are more?'

'I'm thinking of your Albanian friends.'

'The Zamirs?'

'Correct.'

'They're not my friends.'

'I use the word loosely.'

'You know I'm on their black list?'

'You'll soon be off it.'

'What are you thinking of, Colonel?'

'In broad terms, Pezas will plan and co-ordinate the operation, the Zamirs will find a way into the office, you will go in with them and find the documents.'

'What documents?'

'That is the question!'

'Are you sure they exist?'

'Of course they exist! Lazaridis was dealing with highly sensitive material. There's enough dirt in his files to bring any government to its knees.'

'How do I know what to look for?'

'You'll know, Zafiris! That's why I want you. Specifically you! Because you have a nose for these things and you will find them with the certainty and precision of a hunting dog!'

'This is going to be expensive.'

'Undoubtedly. But the prize is great.'

'Have you got the funding?'

'Don't worry about that.'

'But have you got the funding?'

'I have.'

'Good. I'll need 10,000 up front just to get this started.'

Sotiriou stood up, unfolding his angular body like a stork. He took a key from his pocket, lifted a few books from a shelf and placed them on the floor at his feet. He inserted the key into the dark space left by the books. A lock turned. A metal door swung on its hinges. The Colonel's hand emerged with several stacks of 50-euro notes held together with paper bands.

'Have you got a bag?'

Zafiris reached for his briefcase and Sotiriou counted out ten packets of notes.

'Try to keep the Zamirs to a reasonable price,' said the Colonel.

'That won't be easy.'

'If they get silly, tell them I have a big file on them and I'm ready to put them away for fifteen years.'

'Really?'

The Colonel frowned. 'Tell them that. Fear is the only morality we have left these days. Let's use it when we have to.'

'One more question.'

'Go ahead.'

'What protection can you offer?'

The Colonel eyed him steadily. 'You know I can't guarantee anything.'

'You always say that.'

'Because it's true.'

'But *why* is it true?'

'Come on, Zafiris! You know as well as I do. If this was an official operation, I'd give you all the support you want. But this is off the record. I can't be connected to it.'

'I accept that. But we'll need an escape route if this goes wrong.'

The Colonel put his fingertips to his temples and closed his eyes. He seemed to allow a storm to settle in his head. It took a full minute. Opening his eyes again, he said calmly, 'Talk to Pezas. See what he wants. If we can help you – untraceably – we will.'

George closed his briefcase. 'That's more than you've ever offered before, Colonel. I'll let you know.'

He left the police headquarters in an agitated state. Here at last was the money he needed, but so tangled up with risk that his conscience, and his instinct for self-preservation, told him not to touch it. At the same time the calculating part of his brain was doing the sums; stripping out the emotion, the suspicion, listing the key facts, echoing the time-honoured equations: expenses 1950 a month, income 2000, result happiness; expenses 2000 euros a month, income 1950, result misery. And then came a few more key facts, undermining some of the others: this was a commission from the Head of the Violent Crimes Squad. Unofficial, probably illegal, but ethically founded. The complications came in with the Zamirs. How could he justify employing criminals? How would it look if they were caught? The thought was unsettling. There was no conceivable defence.

The argument churned on inside him, tormenting his conscience. As he walked home through the wintry streets around Lycabettus, he barely registered the lights coming on in apartment windows, the shops and cafés glowing like golden caves. Everywhere, he told himself, people were compromised, divided, split between principles and necessity, many in far more trying ways. That man in the café, smoking and staring into space. The girl at the bar, arguing into her phone. Even his son Nick, faced with a choice between unemployment, taking a job abroad, and doing obeisance to that poisonous woman Maria Katramis, whom they all had to flatter because she was rich! Nick would have to decide; and deciding – not between good and evil but between two evils – would be a step towards maturity.

If Nick could do it, surely his father could.

Slowly, by the alchemy of walking, his head cleared. He remembered a line from Aeschylus: *wisdom is the recognition of necessity*. For 'necessity', he reflected, read 'money'.

21

Haris was on the phone early the next morning – pulsing with his trademark 'good energy'.

'*Kalimera*, boss!'

'*Kalimera*, Haris. What's up?'

'Job done!'

'Which job?' George switched his phone to loudspeaker so that he could carry on making coffee. He glanced at the clock: 7.32.

'We got the necklace.'

'You're kidding me.'

'No sir!'

'How much did she pay?'

'Twelve.'

'That's a hell of a discount.'

'Not bad!'

'How did she swing that?'

'No idea.'

'She told you nothing?'

'Nothing. Just went in, came back out, and said "Let's go."'

'Where were you?'

'In the car.'

'And she?'

'In his house.'

'So she went in, stayed a few minutes…'

'Fifteen, twenty minutes.'

'Then she came out…?'

'With the necklace!'

'Why at his house?'

'He didn't want any surprises.'

'Fair enough.'

'Have you seen the place?'

'No.'

'It's a fortress. I've seen military bases less well defended.'

'Did you meet him?'

'Of course.'

'Was he civil?'

'Very.'

'Has he forgiven me?'

'I don't know about that.'

'I don't want to be on some Albanian vendetta list.'

'He knows you didn't shop him to the police.'

'Are you sure?'

'I cleared it up with him.'

'Did you understand each other?'

'Totally.'

'You actually discussed it? Your comradeship of life and death?'

'Not in so many words. But he understands.'

'In that case,' said George, 'I want you to do me a big favour. Call him now and put in a good word for me.'

'Don't worry. He doesn't have a problem.'

'I need something from him.'

'What?'

'It's something we can't discuss on the phone. A project.'

'OK boss. I'll speak to him.'

George lit the flame under the coffee pot. 'Call me when you have an answer.'

Five minutes later, as the little copper *briki* foamed at the brim, he had a second call from Haris. Flamur Zamir was willing to talk, he said. All George had to do was make an appointment. George thanked him and at once rang Zamir. The Albanian was formal, but the resentment had gone from his voice. They agreed to meet at three that afternoon.

George put down the phone, and was about to pour the coffee when Nick walked in, his eyes lighting up at the sight of the full *briki*.

'Is that for me?'

'It wasn't,' said George, 'but let's share it.'

He took a second cup from the rack and divided the coffee between them.

'I had a heavy night,' said Nick, sipping the coffee gratefully.

He had been out with his cousin Pandelís, 'pigging out' at a new restaurant in Plaka which specialised in the foods and wines of the Greek islands. At about two in the morning, all quite drunk, Pandelís told him a secret: his parents were planning to offer Nick a job. Not in engineering, not at first; a clerical post which, if he played his cards right, would evolve into a technical or even executive rôle after a few years. The pay would be very low to start with, but gradually improve.

George asked if he planned to accept. Nick said he had been thinking about it for the rest of the night. Although he wanted to come back to Greece, to be close to friends and family, all the places he loved, he had no wish to be obliged to his cousins. He didn't really know what they would be offering him and he preferred to work for an international firm, at least to start with.

'I'm sure you're right,' said George, 'but can you get a job with an international firm?'

'They have a job fair at the university. Employers come along and do interviews.'

'They recruit there?'

'I believe so.'

George thought about this. Zoe would be sorry, and who knows how Stelios and Maria would react? But did that matter? George felt his son had the right approach. He said so, and Nick was clearly relieved.

'I was afraid you'd give me the old family line.'

'Not me. The whole purpose of a university education is to be free of family constraints. There's no point studying all those years just to stick your head in a noose. But don't fool yourself, Nick. An international firm will be no picnic. They're tough, competitive outfits. They'll expect 100% from you. More if you want to get ahead.'

'I guess so.'

'If you want the easy life, go for the family job. Make your mother happy.'

'No thanks, Dad. I want this experience and I have to get it now. I can always come back to Greece later, but I can't do it the other way.'

'Don't be too sure that Katramis will take you after your time abroad.'

'Really? I'll be more employable.'

'Maybe not. Companies like to mould their workers, catch them young, train them in their culture. Especially the Greek family firms. International experience could even be a threat to them.'

'If they're stupid.'

'Well, maybe they are.'

The kitchen door opened. Zoe came in, kissed Nick, waved to her husband, and said, 'Coffee?'

'I'll make it,' said Nick.

'No, I'll make it,' said George quickly. 'You tell your mother the news.'

'Oh,' said Zoe. 'What news is that?'

George was obliged to watch as Zoe reacted first with joy and then with bewildered anger. He put a cup of coffee down in front of her and she glared at him, asking, 'What do you say to this, George? I hope you've told him it's nonsense.'

'To tell you the truth, I think Nick is doing the right thing.'

'How can it be the right thing to shit on your family? The *only* people you have in the world, the *only* people you can rely on, who never ask for a thing from us!'

'It's not shitting on them to say…'

'It's an insult! After all they've done!'

'What have they done?'

'They've interviewed Nick, encouraged him, found work for him! Do you know how many young people would *kill* for a chance to work with that company? Today! In Greece!

Hundreds! Thousands! And Stelios offers the chance to Nick!'

'It's not what he needs right now.'

'What do you know? You gave up a safe, well-paid job in a bank, the stupidest decision of your life, and you presume to tell your son what to do with his career! That's unbelievable! Really unbelievable.'

'Zoe, I'm not telling Nick what to do.'

'Don't be an idiot, George! Of course you are! You say, "That's OK, my boy, anything you want." But he doesn't know what he's doing. He's still young. He can't see the road ahead as you can. You should guide him. Be a proper father to him! Instead of playing the great liberal.'

'I'm not "playing" anything.'

'That…' she flung an accusing finger and turned to face Nick, 'that is the way to bankruptcy. Look at a man who is about to go bust! Follow his advice if you want to! Join the club!'

George was appalled. Nick was tongue-tied. He shot a wild and fearful glance at his father.

Zoe said, 'If Stelios offers you a job, take it! Understand? It doesn't matter if it's third photocopying clerk in Agrinion, JUST TAKE IT!'

George found his voice. 'Zoe, I would understand if Nick had left school without a degree, or got one of those ridiculous qualifications like show business studies, but he's an engineer! There's a shortage of engineers! He can work anywhere in the world, for some of the best companies – Shell, BP, Schlumberger, Nissan, Rolls-Royce – and you want him to give that up for the sake of working for your cousins in Athens? That is truly idiotic!'

'Oh yes? And where is this wondrous job with Shell or General Electric? Who are his contacts there? Who's offering it?'

'They have job fairs at university.'

'Job fairs, my ass! It all comes down to who you know! That's how it's always been and always will be. Nick, if you turn this opportunity down I will never forgive you!'

Nick closed his eyes.

George intervened again. 'There's a world out there, Zoe, where jobs are earned on merit, and not through nepotism. Nick has escaped our horrible medieval labyrinth of cronyism, he's seen a better way of doing things, and you want to drag him back! Into this filth, this backwardness! Have some thought for him! For his spirit as a man!'

'Oh don't start with all your "spirit" nonsense! You failed, so you want your son to fail too. It's as simple as that.'

'That's bullshit, Zoe.'

'At least my bullshit gets him a job!'

'Not as an engineer.'

'That's how you start. *A foot in the door!*'

'Only in a primeval, ignorant, backward-looking outfit like Katramis! If Nick goes to work for them he'll learn the worst habits, the worst business practices, and after ten years he'll be corrupt, lazy, cynical and *unemployable!* Is that what you want for your son?'

'You don't know what you're talking about, George. Nick, listen to me. Do as I say. You'll be fine.'

Nick raised his hands. 'This is really upsetting me. I'm not even sure it's about me any more.' He stood up. 'Please settle your differences between yourselves. I'll make my own decisions.'

140

He turned and left the room.

Zoe shook her head in disgust. 'Look what you've done now. He won't even talk to us any more!'

'We can't force him.'

'A true father *would* force him!'

'I'm not prepared to ruin my son's future for the sake of the family.'

'You're so full of shit. You seem to forget how Stelios and Maria have helped us.'

'Really?'

'They ask for nothing back.'

'How often has this happened?'

'More and more often.'

'How much?'

'A little at a time, but it adds up.'

'Why didn't you tell me?'

'To protect your feelings.'

'But why? We've been getting by.'

'Only through their help.'

George winced. 'We must pay them back.'

'How?'

'We'll manage it. Work's picking up.'

'It'll have to pick up a hell of a lot!'

'How much are we talking about?'

'I've told you, they don't want anything back.'

'It's a matter of pride, Zoe.'

'Of course it's a matter of pride! How do you think I feel?'

George glanced at the clock.

'I'd better get ready.'

'For what?'

'I'm driving Nick to the airport.'

'Think about what I've said. And when they offer him the job, make damn sure he takes it!'

22

The phone call came as they were driving to the airport. Maria Katramis, her voice syrupy and ingratiating, asking how they all were and saying how very much they had enjoyed seeing Nick. They would like to see more of him, she said, and when he finished his degree, there should be a place for him in the company, a humble one admittedly, but the first step in a long and successful career… George interrupted, unable to bear her wheedlings any longer.

'Maria, I'm driving. Why not speak to him yourself?'

She hesitated, surprised, before the flow resumed. 'I'll do that. But first I want to consult you, George, about a little problem. Maybe you can help?'

'Try me.'

'Is this a good moment?'

'If you make it quick.'

'This is a delicate business, George, and I need total discretion.'

'You can rely on me.'

'I know. That's why I called you. And I like to keep things in the family.'

'What's the problem?'

'We've become aware of a disinformation campaign against us.'

'Who's doing it?'

'A rival company. US based.'

'What are they doing?'

'Spreading rumours in the industry and the political parties. False reviews, accusations, questioning our honesty and fiscal probity…'

'You need a specialist in reputation management.'

'That will be expensive.'

'It's the way to do it.'

'Don't you have any more… let's say, *direct* methods?'

'Like what?'

'I don't know. Something to scare them off?'

'I don't do scare tactics, Maria.'

'You know what I mean.'

'I don't think I do. Look, can we meet and talk about it? I'm taking Nick to the airport, and…'

'All right, but I need this sorted today. How about this afternoon?'

'I have a meeting at three. Shall we say six?'

'Fine. Come to Varsos in Kifissia, the big room at the back. I'll be there.'

'That sounded heavy,' said Nick.

'You know who it was?'

'You called her Maria. Could it be my aunt?'

George nodded. 'When you've graduated they'd like to see more of you, as part of the company.'

'Then she went on to something else.'

'She wants my help.'

'So that's the kickback. We offer Nick a job; in return you fix our problem.'

'That's about it.'

'Make sure they pay you.'

'I will.'

'Is it true about being bankrupt?' Nick seemed embarrassed.

'No. It's been a hard few years, but things are OK.'

'Mother gave you a hard time about that.'

'I'm used to it.'

'Anyway,' Nick's tension vanished, 'with luck I'll be off your books by June.'

'That's fine,' said George.

They talked of other things – Nick's approaching exams, his dissertation on fuel-saving solutions for cargo ships, his feelings about reaching the end of his studies. All too soon they were on the big right-hand curve off the Attiki Odos that swung towards Koropi and the airport, with jets descending on the glide path overhead. This was always a sad moment. The end of the holidays. Soon they would separate, and the companionship, the relaxed unspoken understanding between father and son, would be broken off. George realised that he had been feeling high for the three days of Nick's visit. Now he could see a darker state of mind approaching, like a big grey cumulus looming on the horizon. Nothing could be done to stop it. The time must come, and he must endure it.

He parked in the drop-off lane. Nick said, 'Don't come in with me, Dad. It only prolongs the pain.'

'I hope you're not sad, Nick.'

'No. Only when I think of you and mother quarrelling.'

'We'll try to put a stop to that.'

'I would love that.'

Nick gave his father a long hug, lifted his rucksack onto his back, and was off through the glass doors of the terminal building. George watched him go, marvelling at the innocent optimism, the energy, the alertness, that strange mix of physical perfection and naïveté – precisely that inability to see 'the road ahead' as Zoe called it, with its consequences, responsibilities and complications – which kept the vision clear, the skies of hope cloudless. As young men went, Nick was mature and thoughtful. Part of his training as an engineer, no doubt. But still: the wish that he and Zoe would stop quarrelling – just like that, despite the real substance to their disagreements – seemed hopelessly, almost childishly unrealistic.

23

In the blinding white marble-pillared hall of his house, Flamur Zamir stood smiling presidentially next to an exact copy of himself. The same hawk-like features, the same thin moustache and shoulder length black ringlets, the same loud clothes. For a surreal moment, George thought he was looking at a waxwork statue, so perfect, so still was the likeness. Then Flamur said, 'Meet my brother Fisnik.' The statue offered its hand.

They led him into an equally dazzling *saloni* with pale blue leather sofas arranged in a U around a low table dressed in zebra skin. George's eyes wandered disbelievingly over the décor: a pair of life-size red marble lions reclined sleepily with silk cushions on their backs; in the chimney a log fire blazed under a mural of an ancient warrior driving a chariot past a city wall, dragging a bloodstained lifeless body in the dust.

'Unusual picture,' he said.

'*The Warrior's Triumph*. Achilles parades the body of Hector around the walls of Troy.'

George reflected that money could buy you many things but not good taste. He declined a cup of coffee but accepted a glass of pomegranate juice, which turned out to be the same rich crimson colour as the Zamir twins' trousers.

Haris arrived shortly after, his lively face betraying no reaction to the surroundings. He sat down next to George, nodded to the brothers and said, 'OK boss, tell us about the job.'

George described it as far as he was able. The others listened, then began asking questions. How many guards? Which floor? Other occupants of the building? Offices, or flats?

'I can't answer those questions,' said George. 'You'll have to go and see for yourselves. I just need to know if you're willing to take it on, and how much you'll charge.'

Flamur glanced at his brother, whose left hand, resting on the arm of the sofa, lifted and opened, then settled again.

'Fifty thousand,' said Flamur. 'Possibly more if the job turns out to be complicated.'

'Fifty thousand? That's a hell of lot!'

Flamur was stony-faced. 'That's the price.'

George laughed. 'I've got five to offer you.'

Flamur laughed back, an unnerving, mechanical sound.

'It's one night's work,' said George.

'And maybe five years in prison.'

'Who is this for?'

'I can't give you the name of my client, but I can tell you he's not rolling in money.'

'Forget it,' said Flamur grimly.

'Tell me your lowest price,' said George.

'We've told you the price. It's not the lowest and it's not the highest. If you want a cheap job, go to someone else.'

George took out his phone. 'Let me check.'

Colonel Sotiriou always disliked being called, so George went straight to the point.

'Fifty thousand?' said the Colonel coolly. 'That's steep. Very steep! Is it including yours?'

'No, that's just the Zamirs.'

'How much for you?'

'Twenty-five. Including Haris.'

'This is the police, Zafiris, not the Onassis Foundation!'

'And this is a stinker of a job.'

'All right, tell them to go ahead.'

George ended the call. 'Gentlemen,' he said, 'we're in business.'

Haris and the Zamirs agreed to go down and take a look right away. They promised to have a plan for him within 48 hours.

George drove down through heavy afternoon traffic to Kifissia. He cruised the streets for several minutes in search of a parking place before giving up and resentfully paying five euros to an unshaven man for a slot on an empty building site. A short walk through boutique-lined streets that could have been transplanted from Boston or Paris brought him to No 5 Cassavetes, where the faded primrose light of Varsos – dairy, bakery and café – filtered through plate-glass windows onto the busy pavement. George walked in through the swing doors, between displays of traditional sweets laid out as plainly and unceremoniously as goods in an ironmonger's store: trays of *kataïfi, sokolatina* and *baklavá,* cabinets stuffed with *tsouréki* and rusks, fridges packed with milk puddings and yoghurt, wooden racks holding jams and honey and fruits in syrup, shelves of biscuits, cakes, *petits fours* and meringues. He had always loved this place. Nothing had changed since the 1970s. Neither the merchandise nor the army of motherly serving ladies who scribbled out a chit for every item bought like nurses issuing prescriptions. Even forty years ago, when George first remembered going there, it had felt like a relic of pre-war days, a living museum of the decorous old Greece, with its barber shops smelling of rose-water, its clanking trams, its pomaded shoe-shine men. He would not be surprised to see Venizelos or Cavafy taking tea here, pin-stripe suited ghosts of the 1920s.

Maria Katramis sat at a table in the far corner of the café, prodding at her mobile phone. Her appearance was different from usual: pale and plain, her clothes less showy, the customary festoons of jewellery absent from her arms and throat. George pulled up a chair.

'Hello, Maria.'

She jumped. 'Oh, George, I got such a fright!'

'I'm sorry.'

She offered her cheek, which George kissed lightly.

'What will you have?' she asked.

'Black tea please.'

She signalled to the waiter. 'Two teas here.'

She settled a bitter gaze on George .

'I didn't want to say too much on the phone, Yiorgo *mou*, but I'm worried.'

'About what exactly?'

Her phone rang.

'Excuse me.' She picked it up, checked the name of the caller, and said 'Go to hell' before dropping it back in her bag.

'OK, George, this is strictly between us. Understood?'

'Of course.'

'Nothing must get out. Not even to Zoe.'

'Fine.'

'You know I'm a tax inspector?'

'Yes.'

'I've been doing that for 27 years and I think I know my job.'

'I'm sure you do.'

'So when some little greenhorn shit comes along and tells me I should do it differently, I don't even give them the time of day.'

George nodded understandingly.

'What's happened?' he asked.

'A young lady, educated in Germany, a real smart-ass, is appointed as an "auditor" of our tax office. She starts opening files, looking at procedures, checking our accounts, reading our correspondence and transcripts of telephone calls... Instead of talking to us, getting to know us, how we work as people – because what is an office after all but *people*, with their families, hopes and problems? – instead of doing that, she's obsessed with the rule-book and how we're failing to stick to it. She's put everyone's backs up, but mine more than anybody's because I'm in charge and the responsibility falls on me.'

'Is your job on the line?'

'I don't know. Nobody knows! This government produces a new law every 15 minutes, and of course 90% of these laws are just hot air. They'll never be applied. But of course the European Union is twisting their arms, so once in a while a law *is* applied, and then God help us! They keep saying we have to cut down the number of state employees, and of course that would be a disaster, but one day some jobs will undoubtedly have to go. We try to make sure it's the really useful jobs that get cut – bus drivers, doctors, people on the telephone help lines – so that the public will be inconvenienced and protest…'

'I'm sure you're quite safe.'

'That little German *puttana* has her eye on me. I can sense it!'

'You said there's a rival firm?'

The waiter arrived with their tea.

'Can I smoke?' she asked.

'In the garden, madam. In here it's forbidden.'

'More German rules! Greeks like to smoke. So let us smoke!'

'It's the law, madam, not me.'

'They tyrannise us with their stupid laws. Leave us alone now.'

The waiter placed a ticket under the teapot and moved away.

Maria waited until he was out of earshot.

'There is a rival firm,' she said softly, 'and it's my suspicion that they are subsidising this little tart.'

'What for?'

'To cripple us! They waste my time and energy defending myself from false accusations, and simultaneously discredit our company. Win win!'

George considered this. It was quite plausible. American businesses were notorious for playing dirty with the competition.

'Let me be clear,' said George. 'You're also a director of the construction company?'

'Don't say it too loudly.'

'Why?'

'Come on, George! I'm sure you see nothing wrong in it, but others, the jealous ones, the carpers and complainers, who have no projects of their own, who live only to bring down successful people – they attack us!'

'How much of this is public knowledge?'

'None of it!

'So how are you discredited?'

'Rumours, gossip, black propaganda in the trade.'

'Anything in the press?'

'No, thank God! But who reads the press now?'

'Social media?'

'Nothing yet. But that will be next. Unless we stop it. Which is why I called you in.'

'I'm not the man for social media. You need a 25-year-old.'

'Don't worry. We need to strike deeper than that.'

'You have a plan?'

'It's an idea. Presumably as a private detective you have ways of digging up dirt on people?'

George felt uneasy. 'The dirt has to be there. I don't fabricate it.'

'Of course not. But you know where to find it?'

'I can certainly look in the usual places. Who are you thinking of? The auditor, or the rival firm?'

'Both!'

'Digging costs money, you realise?'

'Naturally. But I hope there's a family discount!'

George had been waiting for this. 'If anything there's a family premium,' he said. 'I don't generally take on any family work.'

'That's crazy.'

'I broke my rule once and regretted it for years after.'

'Am I wasting my time?'

'No. I'll make an exception again, because you've been kind to Nick, kind to us all in fact, but that's the only "discount" you'll get. My rate is 200 a day, plus costs. It's the same for everyone. Non-negotiable.'

'That's a lot of money.'

'If it seems a lot, don't hire me.'

'How do you justify it? When pensions are cut to 600 a month...'

'How much are you paid, Maria?'

'Me? I don't discuss that!'

'Why not?'

'It's none of your business.'

'No problem. I don't really want to know.'

'So why ask?'

'Just to keep things in perspective.'

'What perspective? We're in totally different professions. You can't compare.'

'But the cost of a meal, a house, a pair of shoes, remains the same.'

Maria was indignant. 'I don't know where you're trying to go with this, George, but if I were you I would stop now! If you want this job. If not, carry on with this nonsense...'

'I'm not interested in your finances, Maria. You questioned my fees. Remember, I don't earn every day. You can't say 200 a day multiplied by 30 is my monthly income. It's more like multiplied by six. And that's a good month.'

'You work just six days a month? Lucky you!'

'That's all I'm *paid for.* It's often less.'

She did not seem to have anywhere to put that information. She sat looking awkward and embarrassed.

George said, 'Are we agreed then? 200 a day?'

'That's really the best you can do?'

He nodded.

'How about 150?'

'Maria, I'll be offended if you go on. If you can't afford it, just say so, we'll finish our tea and forget all about it.'

'It's not about affording it!'

'I'll need seven days in advance and all the information you can give me about the targets.'

Maria said no more for a while. She sipped her tea with a thoughtful expression. Eventually she said, 'Perhaps there's a quicker option.'

'What's that?'

'I don't want to say it.'

George at once understood.

'If you don't want to say it, don't. You'll probably regret it.'

'Depends on how you take it. You'd get more money for a lot less work.'

'If it's what I'm thinking, I have two comments. One, it's much more expensive. Two, I don't do illegal, as I've told you before.'

'You've never said that.'

'I'm saying it now.'

She shuffled slightly in her chair and softened her voice. 'I suppose you know people who are prepared...'

'I try to steer clear of those people. The prisons are full of them. And of the fools who hired them.'

'Sometimes it's enough, surely, just to give them a little fright?' She smiled nervously. 'I'm not talking about big things.'

'Little things can go wrong and turn into big things very quickly. That is definitely not my game.'

'You're cunning, George! Right now I happen to know that you are dealing with some Albanians who would certainly know how to put a squeeze on someone…'

George was astounded that she knew this. He did his best to look blank.

'My son told me the whole story,' she said.

'And?'

'Wouldn't they oblige?'

'You can ask them directly.'

'I can't possibly do that! In my position? It has to come from you.'

'It's not going to do that. Forget it.'

Maria eyed him viciously. 'You'll do it for Olli, but not for me!'

George groaned. 'All I did for Olli was help her get stolen property back. No one was hurt or frightened. What you're talking about is totally different.'

'It's just a job! These people handle guns like you and I use a knife and fork!'

'The answer is no.'

She did not appear to hear this. 'Let's say it takes two to three weeks to do it the slow way. That's three to four thousand euros. I'll give you 1,000 just to telephone your Albanian and ask the question. Nothing else. That's not a bad deal.'

'Save the money and call him yourself,' said George. He

slipped the ticket from under the teapot and scribbled Zamir's number on it. He pushed it back across the table at her and stood up.

'Sit down, stupid,' she said.

'I'm going.'

'Please, George!' She flashed him a pleading, almost desperate look. 'I'll pay your fees, and we'll do it your way.'

24

With money in his pocket, George was feeling a great deal better. New energy. Nice energy. Mind and body in harmony. Confidence. Problems solvable.

The weather was warming up too, pushing away the bleak January days, moving gently but surely towards spring. When the *alkyonides* arrived – the 'halcyon days' said by the ancients to be set aside by the gods each February for kingfishers to mate – Zoe's dark mood lifted and she announced that she was going to open up the house in Andros. George welcomed the news. She had been at a dangerous loose end all winter, alternating between depression and savagery, looking interminably for trouble. Once she got out to the island she would start painting seriously and that hideous black energy that pooled inside her would be dissipated, converted into landscapes and still lifes of surprising beauty. It seemed a kind of alchemy.

Armed with the information he needed about the auditor at the tax office and the suspect rival firm, George began his investigations. Complications – never far below the surface – were soon emerging. The 'German girl', in fact a Greek by the name of Sonia Venieri, was highly resistant to his approach. She made him feel like one of those telephone sales people who spend their days cold-calling strangers and trying to engage them in conversation.

'I don't know you,' she said, 'and I don't want to know you.'

When he tried again, she blocked his number. He sent a text message and got no reply. He tried an email. Nothing. Only a Google search for her name produced a few crumbs of information. She had studied at Athens College, then Heidelberg and Cambridge. Since Athens College was his old school, and he still had a good friend on the staff there, Christos Mazis, George called him and asked if he remembered her.

'Sonia Venieri? Vividly,' said his friend.

'Why?'

'She was a star pupil. Head girl, captain of athletics, national prizewinner in maths. A great girl. What every teacher dreams of.'

'Family background?'

'Father and mother professors at the Polytechnion.'

'Politics?'

'They're an old Athenian family. Probably conservative, probably crypto-royalist.'

'Any scandals, any black sheep?'

'What's up, George? Are you working for the press now?'

'No.'

'Why these questions?'

'It's a professional matter.'

'Thanks for being so open.'

'I'm sorry, Christo, I really can't say any more. I just want to know if she's all she appears to be.'

'Definitely.'

'Are you in touch with her or her family?'

'No.'

'Thanks very much. You've been a real help.'

George was no further on. There was only one thing for it now: go down to the tax office and speak to her in person.

As an image of the Hellenic State, the tax building did honest service. Vast, dirty, badly constructed and worse maintained, its echoing vestibule was populated by a crowd of agitated citizens, queuing at windows or sitting, bored and furiously blank, on plastic sofas in corridors. Among them flitted a smaller number of more focussed, purposeful beings: tax advisers and accountants, lawyers and fixers, insiders who knew the system and worked it every day. Occasionally a door would open and an arrogant figure step out, stride past the hopeful eyes of the waiting public, and disappear through another door. These were the potentates, the occupiers of desks, servants for life of the great machine, stranglers of enterprise and hope. Poorly paid, they were fabulously placed for the collection of *rousfeti* – that alternative coinage, more ancient than the drachma, that powered the hidden economy. Some, no doubt, laboured honestly in their dismal task of blocking all endeavour, loyally feeding the behemoth of the state with its daily tonnage of paper and pointless permits. Others took every opportunity to fleece the public with their tricks, forms and spiels. 'Here is your tax bill, madam. I know it's high, but you're in a special category. You can either pay it in full through the official channels, or I can let you have a 30% discount for cash. It's up to you.'

George suspected that Maria, with her expensive wardrobe,

was one of the latter types. There wasn't the slightest whiff of honesty about her. She would probably be offended if you even said the word.

The problem now, in this enormous concrete and neon-lit anthill, was to find an employee named Sonia Venieri. The information desk on the ground floor was besieged. He walked around, enervated by the atmosphere of anguish and suppressed aggression, searching for clues. Then he spotted a cleaner with a mop and bucket coming out of a doorway. Taking a 5-euro note from his pocket he asked his question. 'Third floor, auditor's office,' was the answer.

He climbed the stairs to a silent world. A corridor stretched emptily away, past a row of closed beige doors, to a blank cement wall at the end. This was the third floor. The office must be along here. He set off along the corridor, doors to his left, plate-glass windows to the right with a view to the street far below where traffic moved sluggishly like glue leaking out of a tube. Suddenly a door opened and a pale young man with floppy brown hair, his skin the colour of church candles, challenged him.

'This is not a public area. What do you want?'

'I've come to see one of the auditors.'

'Who?'

'Miss Venieri.'

The man eyed him suspiciously. 'Who are you?'

'I have business with her.'

'Is she expecting you?'

'She should be.'

'Your name?'

'Zafiris.'

'Wait there.'

The man went back through the door. George waited.

Two minutes later the door opened again. A severe and cerebral young woman, with thick black hair tied harshly back, steel-rimmed spectacles and cold grey eyes, stepped angrily out, her ugly brown skirt swirling around her ankles.

'This is harassment!' she cried.

'Not at all,' said George calmly. 'I'm just trying to help you.'

'What are you talking about?'

George began explaining, without naming any names. Venieri impatiently broke in: 'Unless you tell me who sent you I'm not prepared to listen to you any more.'

'I'm not at liberty to tell you that, but it's in your interests to listen.'

'I'll decide that.'

'All right, decide.'

'Right,' she said. 'You will leave the building now, and…' She hesitated, sensing no doubt that she might be harming her own cause. 'All right, Mr whatever your name is, say your piece, and make it quick.'

George disliked her arrogant manner intensely.

'I have no "piece" as you call it. I just want to have a conversation, for your benefit. An exchange…'

'Well get on with it!'

'You've made enemies.'

'That's inevitable.'

'Is it?'

'Of course it is! Is this the great thing you've come to tell me?'

'Look,' said George, 'you keep getting the wrong end of the stick. I know you're an auditor in the tax office, so you're not a normal tax inspector tracking down doctors and lawyers and plumbers who get paid in cash. You're doing internal inspections, presumably on bent tax officials.'

She glared at him. 'Who told you this?'

'Never mind. My point is this, you're doing legitimate work, but somehow you've made enemies.'

'So you're threatening me?'

'No. I think there may be a misunderstanding.'

'Almost certainly not.'

'There could be an innocent explanation for...'

'If there is, I'll find it. Without your help.'

'Unless they get to you first.'

'Who are "they"?'

'Your enemies.'

'As I thought. A threat! You are going to get out of here right now!'

'It's not a threat, damn you!'

'What is it? An invitation to a cocktail party? Don't play with words!'

'I'm not making a threat. I want to open a dialogue.'

'Oh, you have all the soft phrases! A "conversation"! A "dialogue"! You must think I'm an idiot. I see hundreds of people like you every week: middlemen, agents, negotiators, bribe specialists. Some talk smooth, some talk rough. The message is always the same.'

'For an auditor you have an amazing inability to listen.'

'You're wasting your time. Go and tell the person who sent you that the investigations are transparent and correct. They are carried out according to European regulations, in order to save our country from bankruptcy and the cancer of corruption. If your client has anything to confess, let him confess it. He will be treated humanely. Correctly but humanely. We need to clean up this mess, this Augean Stable. His collaboration will be appreciated.'

'Now who's the smooth talker?' said George.

She seemed offended. 'You don't believe me? I have tax inspectors who are already helping me. They're sick of the corruption. They can see where it leads. It saps everything.'

'I'm pleased to hear that,' said George. 'Genuinely.'

She grimaced. 'I very much doubt that. But if there's any truth in what you say, do as I ask. Go back to your client and tell them. The offer is there.'

George remembered Maria's wheedling. Her hints at violence. "Give them a little fright…"

'We're dealing with greedy people,' he said. 'People who have lost all sense of civic duty, people who could turn nasty. You realise you are threatening a whole way of life?'

'This is a criminal activity, not some harmless folk tradition! It's on a massive scale. We need to stop it. And we will.'

'Unless they manage to scare you off.'

'That won't help. The system itself will catch them.'

'It hasn't so far, in 200 years.'

'If it isn't fixed, the country's finances will collapse.'

'They have already, haven't they?'

'Not quite. The Europeans are on the case. They know what's going on. They're not fools.'

'OK, I get all that. But we're talking about something more primitive here. Personal power. Greed. Old habits of mistrust and dishonesty that go back to the Turkish occupation and the strategies that people *had to* develop in order to survive.'

'All that has to go! The Turks were kicked out in 1821!'

'But public finances remain a fabulous trough for the pigs to get their snouts into. And don't think the European Union is innocent either! There's plenty of old style piggery there. But Greece is a special case. Because the political parties get loans from a public bank to subsidise everything, and the bank is staffed entirely with political appointments, you can fudge, and lie, and steal as long as you please.'

'No!' she cried. 'It has to end!'

Near breathless with anger, high colour in her cheeks, there was a passion in her that George admired. He wished he wasn't employed to talk her out of her high principles. This was dirty work.

The door opened. The young man with waxy skin was standing there, twitching. He gave George an injured look.

'Miss Venieri,' he said, 'the meeting is about to begin. It's already ten minutes late. Are you coming?'

'Yes of course. One minute and I'm done.'

The man stood his ground.

'What's the problem?' she said.

'We'll go in together.'

'No. You go in. Tell them I'll be there right away.'

The man frowned and turned away, leaving the door open behind him. Miss Venieri reached out and closed it.

'Go back to your client,' she said. 'Tell him or her to act quickly. Things are moving fast here.'

She offered her hand. 'I must go.'

'Thanks for your help.'

165

Her eyebrows rose. 'Thank you – I hope – for yours.'
She turned and walked quickly away.

George went thoughtfully down the stairs, replaying the conversation. It had not been easy, and he was surprised to find himself thinking with a certain grudging respect of Miss Venieri. She had conviction, intelligence and maturity. She had not given an inch. She would make a formidable enemy. He almost believed her mission might succeed.

25

Outside the frenzied ant-heap of the tax office, he decided to walk towards the centre of town, for the exercise and the chance to think. The pavements of Athens are not usually a good place for thinking, with their ever-changing sea of obstacles, weirdos, beggars, lunatics, badly parked cars and rubbish bins, the shops intriguing or preposterous, the cinemas with giant billboards and the actors' names transcribed comically into Greek – Tzonny Ntep, Tzoud Lo, Kira Naïtely, Kim Mpazintzer – the bars and cafés, the *ouzeris* and *mezedopoleia,* all animated by that restless, chaotic Athenian energy that burns in the air and in the souls of the citizens and drives them to extremes of brilliance and folly. Sometimes, however, the very craziness of the scene produces its own monotony, and George found he was able to think with surprising clarity.

From having too little to do, he suddenly had too much. There was the raid on the Lazaridis office to be planned, the 'rival firm' to look into for Maria Katramis, and a discussion to be had with Maria about the implacable Miss Venieri and her moral crusade. Behind it all, waiting in the shadows, was that long-deferred business with Wasim Khan. It was high time he did something about that, but with no money to move it forward, the cause of the battered Pakistani seemed stuck forever at the back of the queue. As soon as he had half a day free, he resolved to devote time to it.

Next morning he began on his list of calls. First was Haris, who said that he and Zamir planned to visit the Lazaridis office building that afternoon. They would talk again at five when they had a clear idea of the layout, entry and exit routes, the security arrangements generally.

George turned his mind next to the rival construction firm that was bothering Maria. With help from former banking colleagues he discovered it to be the subsidiary of an American company, ICP (Iron Cage Projects), which operated in a number of countries, most of them troubled. In the last two years Iron Cage had won several contracts in the harshly competitive Greek public sector, undercutting Katramis by a big margin. Their prices were well below the market rate. They were clearly using spare cash to subsidise discounts that would put local contractors out of business. There were five directors listed, three Americans and two Greeks. One of the Greeks was a politician, the other a shipowner. Everything George heard about their business methods he disliked, and he even began to feel a certain sympathy for Maria and Stelios. When he rang the Athens office, a Greek-American with an abrasive voice, Jerry Kasimatis, answered the phone.

'Nobody's doing anybody any favours,' he said. 'And nobody's asking. This is a very very tight market.'

'No doubt,' said George. 'But more cooperation and less aggression might ease the situation for you both.'

'Forget it. We're two lions drinking from the same

water-hole.'

'I'm sorry you see it like that.'

'I'll bet you are!'

'There are major interests at work here.'

'Tell me a city where there aren't.'

'Could we meet and talk about it?'

'What's the point?'

'They're asking you nicely this time. Next…'

'Don't try that one on me, buddy! I come from New York. We wrote the book on that stuff.'

'I'm not talking about "that stuff"…'

'We're *only* talking that stuff!'

'I promise you…'

'Don't bullshit me, Zafiris! Your friend Katramis knows the rules. He's bullied and bribed his way with the worst of them. Now he wants to be a *gentleman*? That's a big fucking joke.'

'Why don't you talk to him? Maybe you could work something out.'

'Like what? The terms of surrender?'

'You're being very crude.'

'Life is crude! Haven't you noticed?'

'Who's behind you?'

'Mind your own business.'

'I'm curious why an American company would invest in this messed up country…'

'You're curious? Well guess what, you just answered your own question.'

'What do you mean?'

'You know anything about business?'

'Something.'

'OK. Think about it. And don't bother calling when you've figured it out.'

And that was it: 'Call ended'.

George wondered if Maria knew what she was up against.

He called her and she answered briefly, in a hectic mood.

'Not now, *Yiorgaki mou,* I'm drowning in work. Call me this afternoon. Or better this evening.'

She hung up.

Annoyed, George rang back. He got her answering service.

'Listen, Maria, I'm not going to call back later, because believe it or not I'm busy too. My message is simple. Jerry Kasimatis is a tough customer. You won't get anywhere negotiating with him. Call me if you want more.'

Suddenly the day was offered to him. Nothing to do till late this afternoon. He walked up the road to the garage and picked up the car.

Nea Makri, on the coast near Marathon, had the desolate frontier atmosphere of a seaside town in the off season, as if the few remaining inhabitants, rattling loosely about in spaces too big for them, were guarding the place between invasions. George drove slowly down the long main street, checking the cafés as he went. The All Day Chroma Café on Plastiras Square seemed the best of a dreary lot. He parked nearby, walked in and ordered a *metrio* from the red-haired girl behind the counter.

'Sit down, I will bring it to you,' she said in a heavy Russian accent, her face stony with boredom.

A scattered collection of old men sat wearily about, staring into space – impassive, with hooded eyes, thinking

170

mysterious thoughts. Foreign observers, seeing these white moustaches, these level gazes, were inevitably reminded of ancient philosophers. As if Plato, Aristotle, Pythagoras, those endlessly fertile minds, would have spent their lives lounging about in cafés! Grinding through years of idleness and tedium, doing nothing! At the bar a couple of more youthful customers, electricians in dungarees, rolled cigarettes and smoked, discussing football and eyeing the Russian girl. No one looked quite right for what George had in mind. He sipped his coffee and waited.

For half an hour nothing happened. The electricians left and no one came in. George finished his coffee and wondered what to do next. He did not have it in him to sit and stare for hours like the old fellows around him. Perhaps he had chosen the wrong café, or the wrong day. He was standing up to leave when a commotion started outside. Dogs barking, heavy boots, shouts. The door swung open and two hunters in military camouflage kit, leading a quartet of mastiffs, swept in with a blast of cold air and the scents of marsh, mud and forest in their slipstream. Big, muscular men, bushy-bearded and wild-haired. They greeted the old men as they entered, clomped up to the bar, and ordered beer and *peynirli,* telling their dogs to lie down. With their loud voices and ready laughter they appeared untouched by the gloom of the past decade.

A political discussion started. One of the old men said, 'If you were Tsipras I'd say "I don't see the difference between you and Samaras. You're milking the system, just like he did, with all your friends and family".'

'If I was Tsipras,' said one of the hunters, 'I'd say go to hell. Who are you? Nobody!'

'But you're supposed to be a communist. Everybody should be equal. Even you, Mr Tsipras!'

'Equal?' The hunter laughed. 'Me? I'm the Prime Minister!'

'Communist, capitalist you're all the same. Get into power and help yourself!'

George asked the hunters if they knew any of the landowners round there.

'Oh yes. We know them. Not sure they know us, but we know them!'

'I'm looking for the one that owns the land opposite the *Thalassaki* taverna.'

The hunter exchanged a glance with his companion. 'That's Yerakas,' he said.

'I know a Simeon Yerakas,' said George, remembering a silver-haired property developer whom he had clashed with in the past. 'He builds hotels and tourist resorts.'

'That's the one.'

'He lives there?'

'His son runs the place.'

'What the son's name?'

'Sevastianós.'

'Chip off the old block, is he?'

'No way.' He waggled his little finger with contempt. 'He's a daddy's boy.'

'Does he let you hunt on his land?'

'Probably not.'

'Why probably?'

'He doesn't know.'

'He has guards, surely?'

'We know them all.'

172

'Does he have Pakistanis working there too?'

'Poor sods.'

'Why do you say that? He gives them work.'

'It's not work. It's slavery.'

'I heard one died.'

'Only one?'

'How does that happen?'

'He doesn't pay them for months. When they protest, the sticks come out.'

'Surely that can't go on?'

'What is it to you?'

George had to answer carefully. 'I knew one of them. He was a friend. I thought of going to the police.'

'Good luck to you.'

'Don't waste your time,' said the other. 'Yerakas is a big shot. He'll have you for breakfast.'

'Where does he live?'

'He has a lot of houses.'

'I'm talking about here.'

'Along the road to Marathon. After three kilometres, there's a farm road up to the left, between tall trees. At the end you come to a big white house with guards, fences, floodlights. Like a prison.'

'Doesn't sound very welcoming.'

'It's not.'

George chatted a while longer about other things, then paid the bill and left. He went back to his car and set off towards Marathon.

After three kilometres a dirt road appeared on the left,

climbing between tall trees as the hunters had said. He turned
up it and followed it for another two kilometres into wooded
hills. At a bend in the road a large metal gate barred the way.
A video camera on one of the gate posts watched him arrive,
switch off his engine and step cautiously out of his car. He
approached the gate, found a bell-push and pressed it.

A metallic voice answered. 'Yes?'

'George Zafiris, private investigator. Is Mr Yerakas there?'

'Is he expecting you?'

'No.'

'What do you want?'

'I want to talk to him.'

'Everybody wants to talk to him.'

'This is a serious matter. About a crime committed on his
land.'

'What crime?'

'I'm not going to talk to a gatepost.'

'What crime?'

'If Mr Yerakas won't talk to me, the next visit will be from
the police.'

'What crime?'

'Murder.'

'When was this?'

'A month ago.'

'I don't know anything about it.'

'Just tell Mr Yerakas I'm here.'

George stood at the gate and waited, contemplating the
concrete road that started underneath it and ran through the
woods around the shoulder of the hill. To the right and left
a high chain-link fence snaked away among the bare trees.

There were video cameras at 15-metre intervals.

He heard the sound of an engine. A jeep came bumping down the concrete road, two men on board. The passenger, a tough guy in a cheap black suit, stepped out. He adjusted his broad shoulders as he approached the gate, checking George over with a cold security guard's eye.

'What's this about?'

'I need to speak to Mr Yerakas. Personally.'

'He doesn't talk to strangers.'

'He needs to talk to me.'

'And you need to talk to *me* before you can talk to him.'

'I've told you what this is about.'

'What's it got to do with Mr Yerakas?'

'A workman was killed on his land.'

'I never heard about it.'

'The man died in hospital. He was a Pakistani.'

'Nothing to do with us.'

'It's very much to do with you. And Mr Yerakas. He needs to answer some questions.'

'Are you police?'

'I work under contract for them.'

'Got a card? Proof of identity?'

George handed over a business card. The man read it, flipped it over, pursed his lips.

'Private detective? With a red Alfa Spider?'

'Any objections?'

'It's weird.'

'What kind of car do you expect me to drive?'

'Four by four. X5, Range Rover, Shogun. Even a Hummer.'

'Tinted windows? Bulletproof?'

'Yeah, why not?'

'That's not for me.'

The man sniggered. 'And that old thing is?'

'She's an old friend, and a lot of fun.'

The man said no more. He pulled a phone from his pocket and punched in a number. A few words were exchanged and the call ended. He nodded to the driver of the car and the gate opened.

'Shall I follow you?' said George.

'No. Open the passenger door. I'll ride with you.'

26

They pulled up in front of an ugly white house. Someone had struggled once to make it pretty with urns, trellises and climbing plants, but it had been a losing battle. The barred windows, aluminium doors and large expanses of dirty pebble-dash gave the place a brutally paranoid atmosphere.

They entered through a service door and George was led along a low-ceilinged corridor to a bunker-like office where a man in his thirties, expensively dressed, handsome yet troubled, was speaking agitatedly on the telephone in English.

'I'm doing what I can!' he said. 'You know what it's like. Everything's a fight. And he doesn't like to lose.'

Ignoring George, he listened to the reply. 'OK, I hear you,' he said. 'You're right. In principle. But I'm trying to deal with realities. I'm sorry, I have to go now. Enjoy New York. See you soon. Lots of love.'

He put down the phone. 'Excuse me,' he said, switching to Greek, which was as flawless as his English. He rose from his chair and shook hands. 'Sebastian Yerakas. How do you do? I understand you're a detective.'

'I prefer to be called an investigator.'

'OK, not sure what the difference is, but "investigator" it

is.' He glanced at the suited man who had brought George in. 'You can leave us, Mihali.'

George waited as Mihali left the room.

The young man's face resumed its troubled look.

'There's been a death? Tell me.'

'One of your farm workers. A man called Wasim. Do you know who I mean?'

Yerakas looked vague. George showed him the photo of Wasim taken on his death bed.

'I'm afraid I don't know these men individually.'

George described the scene in the car park a few weeks ago. Yerakas listened carefully. He had a cultivated, open manner, which George found pleasant and surprising. He was as different as could be from his father, Simeon Yerakas, whom George had met once: an arrogant, impatient, menacing man.

'I knew nothing of this,' said Sebastian Yerakas. 'What a horrible tale!'

'It's happening on your land, Mr Yerakas, and in your name.'

'But why? That's what I don't understand.'

'Wasim told me he was not paid.'

'Are you sure of that?'

'It's what he said.'

'The workers on our farms are paid.'

'Have you *seen* them being paid?'

'What, physically?'

'Physically, yes!'

Yerakas smirked. 'One doesn't have to see something happen to know that it happens.'

'How do you know these men are paid?'

'Because no farm could operate without labour, and no labourers will work without wages. Simple as that.'

'I agree. But something went wrong on your farm. Who pays the men?'

'The farm manager.'

'Is he here?'

'I don't know.'

'Can we find out?'

Again the vague look. Yerakas pushed his hands through his hair.

'Well?' George insisted. 'Why not ask that guy in the suit who brought me in? He seems to know what's going on.'

'This is tricky,' said Yerakas.

George waited to see if he would say any more. Eventually the young man lifted his head. 'If you knew what...' He stopped, apparently blocked by some difficult thought.

'Are you in charge here?' asked George.

'Why do you ask?'

'I would expect the owner of an estate like this to have his eye on every detail.'

The young man's eyebrows arched in surprise. 'You would expect that, I know. One hundred percent. There are circumstances here, however, which...' He got lost again in some mental impasse.

'If you're in charge,' said George, 'you'd better start showing it.'

Yerakas looked up sharply. 'What do you mean?'

'If you're the boss, act like the boss.'

'We have a number of businesses. Farms, tourist developments, commercial property. I can't focus too much

179

on the detail.'

'Well, guess what? You're going to have focus on the detail now.'

'Why?'

'You're about to be prosecuted for murder.'

'But I know nothing about it!'

'That's the whole problem. You don't know and you don't care!'

'But I do care! I'm horrified by… What do you mean, I'll be prosecuted?'

'Exactly what I say. I'll go back to the police and give my report. I'll tell them this place is out of control, in the hands of criminals. The next thing you know, buddy, you'll be under arrest. Then, perhaps, you'll focus on the details!'

'I don't want that to happen.'

'Damn right you don't.'

'How do we… how do we prevent this?'

'Show some responsibility. Go down to the farm, find out what the hell happened to Wasim. Who beat him up and why. Report back to me. I'll deal with it after that, with the police.'

'I'd rather you…'

'No! Get down there and find out. Or you'll be the one going to prison. And another thing while you're down there: if there's a grievance about pay, redress it. Before all this happens again.'

Yerakas looked appalled.

'Do you ever go to the farm at Marathon?' asked George.

'From time to time.'

'You should be there three times a week. Minimum.'

Yerakas pulled a face. 'It's not my favourite place.'

'You'll like it even less if you go to prison for this murder.'

'I had nothing to do with it! Can't you see that?'

'You'll have Marathon on your tombstone if you don't sort this out.'

'But how? How do I begin to sort this out?'

'Go down there now.'

'Really?'

'Damn right!'

Yerakas cast his eyes hopelessly around the papers on his desk. 'I'm in the middle of something.'

'Everyone is always in the middle of something! This needs dealing with now! Come on, I'll give you a lift down in my car. Let's take Mihali too.'

'Why?'

'Strength in numbers.'

Yerakas picked up the phone. 'Mihali, please come in.'

He took a last agonised glance at his desk and stood up.

Ten minutes later they were pulling into the taverna car park.

'This is it,' said George. 'Wasim came stumbling in from over there.'

'Why did you get mixed up in it?' asked Yerakas.

'When you see a man with blood all over his face, what do you do? Walk away?'

'Not everyone would intervene.'

'Bugger "everyone".'

George pointed towards the fields on the far side of the road. 'That's your land, I believe?'

Yerakas glanced at Mihali, who nodded.

He doesn't even know his own land, thought George.

181

'Let's go.'

They started picking their way over the furrows of a ploughed field. After 150 metres George noticed the men at work. In a line across the field, a dozen dark figures bent double, cutting handfuls of rocket and dropping them into plastic baskets. At the far end of the line stood a stocky figure with a big alsatian on a leash. Mihalis called out. 'Hey, Manolis!'

The patrolling figure looked up sharply as the dog barked and pulled at the leash. He yanked the dog back, cast an eye over the workers, and began to approach. Seeing him pass, one of the workers straightened up and stretched. The supervisor's head spun round and he shouted, 'Keep working!' before putting on a smile for his boss.

'Good morning, sir! How are we today? Beautiful day! You've come to see the fields. It's all going well. Great crop. People love rocket. It's fashionable now – good for the health – you'll make good money from this.'

'Tell the men to take a break,' said Yerakas.

'We'll do that in a little while – let them keep working or they'll get lazy!'

'Let them have a break – now!'

'Whatever you say, boss!'

He turned and shouted to the workmen. 'Break now! Ten minutes.'

Instantly the men stood up and stretched. A few of them fumbled cigarettes from trouser pockets and sent thin ribbons of smoke into the blue sky.

'I want to talk to you about an incident.'

'What kind of incident?' Manolis looked puzzled.

'About a month ago one of these Pakistanis was killed.'

'Really? Where was that ?'

'Right here.'

'Here?' The words were echoed incredulously. 'Who told you about this?'

Yerakas indicated George.

The supervisor's face hardened. 'Who are you?'

'I'm a private investigator.'

'Huh.' He seemed even more puzzled than before. 'What business do you have on this land? We do our work, we don't bother anybody, what do you want here?'

'He told me the most horrible story,' said Yerakas. 'A man called Yasim…'

'Wasim,' said George.

'…came from here towards that fish taverna over there, covered in blood, beaten up – he was dying as it turned out.'

'Ah,' the light of understanding dawned in Manoli's face. 'I remember now. It was that fight we had, these guys were attacking each other, they got vicious, you know what they're like – they have knives, you can't get near them, they can kill you! Anyway this guy got it in the neck. What do you expect? They're animals.'

'That's not the story he told. Apparently it was about pay.'

'Yes, they were fighting about pay. Or about women! Or cigarettes! I don't know what.'

'No. They were not fighting among themselves. They came to you for their pay and apparently you beat them up.'

'You believe this shit?' He took a long hard look at George.

'You should speak more courteously,' said Yerakas.

'We speak sincerely. Directly. We're all family here. Except people like this who come to cause trouble! What are

183

you after? Money?' He dug his free hand into a pocket and pulled out a €10 note, which he threw on the ground. 'Take it!' he said. 'Take it and piss off!'

George met the man's angry gaze. 'Why don't you answer the question?'

'What question? I never heard a question!'

'Did you refuse that man his pay? Did you then attack him when he came to protest?'

'I've told you! These are animals. Snakes. They fight over anything. They don't know any better.'

'Did you refuse to pay him?'

'Why would I do that?'

'Answer the question!'

'I've told you! This is bullshit.'

'Right,' said George. 'Since you won't answer, let's ask some of these fellows here.'

The supervisor bridled. 'This is none of your business!'

'I'd like to speak to them myself,' said Yerakas mildly.

'Hold on a moment, sir! You know the system here.'

'What system?'

'The family employs me. I employ the farm workers.'

'So? I'm family.'

'You are, of course, but the *head* of the family, Mr Simeon, your father, is the one that I deal with on the farm.'

'He's a busy man. He has delegated me to do this. In fact, legally speaking, I'm the owner of this land.'

'I'm not a lawyer, sir. All I know is the system. Your father gives orders to me and I organise everything.'

'My father would be extremely displeased if he found that you'd been cheating these men out of their wages.'

184

The supervisor smiled unpleasantly. 'Your father always behaves like a gentleman.'

'I'll talk to him,' said Yerakas.

'Fine. He'll explain better than me.'

'The workers will explain better than anyone,' said George.

'You again! What's your problem? Are you a communist?'

'Let me talk to them,' said Yerakas.

'I can't allow that.'

'What do you mean?'

'They're my employees.'

Yerakas pushed past him, irritated. The supervisor glared at George.

'You're in trouble,' he hissed.

George followed Yerakas across the field, the supervisor a few paces behind. The workmen watched suspiciously as they approached. Yerakas introduced himself. George heard the supervisor speaking on his phone.

'Mr Simeon, sir, sorry to bother you but your son Mr Sebastian is here on the farm with a private detective, asking questions and causing trouble... Yes, sir, one moment.'

He called out, 'Mr Sebastian! Your father's on the phone.'

Yerakas took the phone and said irritably, 'Yes, father?'

His troubled look returned and deepened. He seemed to wilt as his father spoke. As if some withering fire was being directed at him.

He tried at one point to object, 'If this is true...' He was silenced at once.

The hectoring continued until all resistance ceased.

'Yes, father, I understand,' he said, and handed back the phone.

He turned to George. 'We're not going to get anywhere like this.'

'So you're not in charge of the farm,' said George. 'Your father is.'

'Apparently!'

'What did he say?'

'A lot of things. Basically, stay out of it.'

'It's what I told you,' said the supervisor complacently. 'We have a system.'

'Let's see how the police like your system,' said George sharply.

He went on: 'If you're the legal owner of this land, you'll be prosecuted. Not your father, not Manolis. You.'

He caught an expression of surprise on the young man's face before a sudden shattering blow hit the back of his head and a rolling red mist exploded through his eyes. He staggered, unseeing, clutching at empty space and felt himself falling towards the ground.

27

George woke up, turned his head with difficulty, and saw that he was lying where he had fallen, in a field of rocket, with its sharp, green, mustardy odour filling his nostrils. There was no one about. Yerakas, the supervisor, Mihalis, the workmen – all gone. He felt in his pocket for his car keys. Still there. With a sense of relief he closed his eyes and slept again.

A little later he came back to consciousness. Unsteadily, feeling stiff and light-headed, he stood up. He could see the fish taverna at the bottom of the slope, his red Alfa Romeo still in the car park. Where had everyone gone? The thought came and went. It did not seem important now. He had other things to deal with. But what? His thoughts were strangely blank. They flickered, unsettled, whited out. Should he go home? See a doctor? Something like that. It was hard to think with a throbbing head.

Putting one foot in front of the other by a conscious effort, he moved haltingly across the field. His limbs felt disconnected from his mind, as if they were moved by someone else's command, like a puppet. He came to the road. Checked four times if it was clear. Crossed it fearfully, despite its emptiness. Reached the car park. Got to the Alfa. Leaned on it gratefully.

Pulled the keys from his pocket.

Sitting in the driver's seat with a pulsing headache he wondered if it was safe to drive. He rather thought not. He closed his eyes to consider the matter better. The darkness felt much gentler than the light.

A while later he woke up with his phone ringing. He fumbled for the 'answer' symbol. The voice that spoke was not a pleasant one.

'This is a warning, Zafiris. Keep out of our business. Leave Marathon and don't come back.'

That was it. No name, number withheld, message delivered. No prizes for guessing who it was.

He turned the ignition key and listened to the engine bursting into life. It seemed miraculously busy and noisy. All those contained explosions in the cylinders, petrol streaming and vaporising, sparks and pistons jumping, crankshaft and camshaft whirring – while for him it was an effort just to move his head. Taking great care, he put the car into gear, eased off the clutch, and drove slowly to Nea Makri. He parked in Plastiras Square and walked unsteadily into the All Day Chroma Café, where he ordered a fresh orange juice and a toasted sandwich. In the bathroom he washed the dirt off his face and hands, splashed water on the nape of his neck, pushed his fingers through his hair, and felt cautiously at the back of his head for damage. The junction of neck and skull felt painful and damp. His fingers returned to him daubed in soil and sticky blood.

Thinking, *I'm doing this for nothing and nobody. For a man who's already dead. Who can't even thank me. Why?* He stared into his own eyes, trying to fathom his thoughts and impulses. Wasim was dead. So who was this for? Risking his life for the sake of what? Those twelve men in the field? Would they thank him? Or would they maybe prefer to keep working, even for miserable wages? There was no easy answer to that.

Back in the café he crunched slowly through the toast, sipping the juice and negotiating an uncertain passage through the haze of memory. His phone gave a silvery tinkle, a message coming in. He ignored it.

Zoe would be angry with him. Angrier than she was already at everything. She would say the self-evident thing. Don't work for nothing! Or for nobody! But this was about principle. The right to life. 'Life, liberty and the pursuit of happiness'. It should be the state that guaranteed those rights, not him, George Zafiris, working single-handed. Having suffered violence himself, he should, for a start, go and denounce those bastards to the police.

He was puzzled about Sebastian Yerakas. Everything he said and did, right up to the moment when the truncheon smashed into his skull, had suggested that he was a reasonable man, possibly even with a conscience. He had probably not landed the blow, to be fair, but even if he had witnessed it without objecting he was guilty of collusion, or some such semi-crime. It scarcely mattered what. He would report the incident and let the police handle it as they wished.

Feeling a little better, he paid the bill and made for his car. Only then, sitting in the driver's seat, did he check his phone to see who had sent him a message. 'Call me,' it said. 'Sonia Venieri.'

He dialled the number. She picked up at once.

'Venieri.'

'Zafiris.'

'I have a question.'

'Fire away.'

'I assumed that was just bullshit from you about helping me?'

'Not at all.'

'You never explained.'

'You never gave me a chance.'

'Tell me now.'

'On the phone?'

'Why not?'

'I would prefer face to face.'

'All right. I'll see you in the café opposite the tax building in five minutes.'

'That's not possible. I'm in Nea Makri.'

'Nea Makri? In winter? What on earth are you doing there?'

'Business.'

'When can you get here?'

'An hour from now.'

'Good. Call me when you arrive. I'll be straight down.'

George drove carefully into Athens, got lucky with a parking spot, and walked into the café at three pm. He called Miss Venieri, who strode in angrily a couple of minutes later. She sat down opposite George and brought her fist down hard on the table. With her fierce green eyes fixed on him she opened her hand. A pair of shiny bullets jostled each other in her palm.

'Did you send these?' she demanded.

'No.'

'Who did?'

'I don't know.'

'Of course you know!'

George shrugged his shoulders.

'Someone sent you to threaten me,' she said.

'Really? I'm not aware of it.'

'Don't play the innocent with me! You've practically said it!'

'Honesty is like tennis, Miss Venieri. It takes two.'

'Of course,' she said. 'But somebody has to serve.'

'The ball's in your court,' said George.

She flicked a strand of hair off her brow.

'Are you sure?'

'I gave you the opportunity,' said George.

'We have rules of disclosure. I can't just discuss my work with the first stranger that comes along.'

'Understood.'

'So let's try again.'

'How many of your colleagues are under investigation?'

She shook her head.

'More than one? Five? Ten?'

'Why do you want to know?'

'Someone sent you those bullets. I'm trying to narrow the field of suspects from the entire staff of the…'

'I understand that!' she said brusquely. 'I'm not an idiot.'

'So how many is it?'

She glared at him. 'Hold on, Mr Detective! I ask the questions! This…' – she held out her hand with the bullets in it – 'is a threat. Intimidation of a public official. A criminal act. By someone who is trying to cover up further criminal acts. Someone who is paying you. I want you to give me the name of that person because I'm going to put them in prison. You too if you don't co-operate!'

George shook his head. 'You'd make a lousy investigator, Miss Venieri.'

'Why do you say that?'

'You jump to conclusions like a firecracker.'

'Stop trying to divert me. It may mean nothing to you, but corrupt officials like the one that sent you cost the Greek State billions of euros each year. This is money that you and I pay from our taxes. Most people are too stupid to see this but…'

'You're also, I might add, extremely arrogant.'

'For me this is not just a job but a duty to my – Why do you say arrogant? What right have you to say that?'

'It's obvious. If you can't see it you never will.'

'I resent that!'

'You talk about people as stupid, you take the first thought that comes into your head as the truth, you're self-righteous, and, what's worst of all, you're so obviously screwed up with your own problems that you…'

'What?' she exclaimed. 'What the hell did you say?'

'I said you're self-righteous. In 99 cases out of 100 that highly unpleasant attitude is caused by guilt.'

'I do not have a sense of guilt!'

'Really? Is that why you dress like a schoolmistress from the 1950s?'

She glared at him. 'That is offensive!'

'I can't be the first to see something bizarre in the way you present yourself. A beautiful…'

'It's none of your business how I present myself!'

'Perhaps not.'

'You want me to look like the other girls on the street, with lipstick and make-up, tight jeans and an unbuttoned shirt? Showing half their breasts? Like a little American tart?'

'It might make more sense.'

'Suppose I don't like the way you dress? You want me to tell you about it? In fact you look pretty shitty to me!'

George held up his hands.

She went on. 'You know what, Mr Zafiris? You're the arrogant one! Like all men, you think you own women, that we exist entirely for your pleasure, that you can patronise us as much as you like. Next you'll be telling me you want to sleep with me!'

'The thought never crossed my mind.'

'Good!'

'Please,' said George, 'accept my apologies. I've spoken badly. If we may, I'd like to get back to business.'

'Then cut out the personal comments.'

'Gladly. I have plenty of good things to say too, but I don't want to irritate you any further.'

She raised her eyebrows in disdainful surprise.

'Neither of us has time to waste,' she said. 'Let's get on with it. Who's your client?'

'I can't tell you that.'

'I think I know anyway.'

George said nothing.

She went on. 'I have a strange job, Mr Zafiris. Very strange. Investigating my own colleagues. Can you imagine that?'

'Uncomfortable, I should think.'

'To put it mildly! I work in an atmosphere of mistrust and fear. I think the worst of everyone, and everyone thinks the worst of me. The tension is horrible. It has a cost.'

'Of course. I understand. But what are you trying to tell me?'

'I want you to see my point of view…'

'I see it.'

'…So that you will let me carry on my work in peace.'

'You're part of a team, I take it?'

'Of course. But the team is small. And underfunded. And fragmented. I suspect we've been set up to fail. A token organisation to fulfil the bailout agreement with our lenders.'

'What makes you think that?'

'There's no leadership.'

'Someone must be in charge.'

'A superannuated old dinosaur from the accounts department. He has no concept of management. He focusses on the formalities, but not on the content, on the substance of what we do.'

'You seem very demanding.'

'I am.'

'You believe in what you're doing?'

'Totally.'

'So why… why not tell me…?'

George stopped, uncertain how to go on. He blinked, trying to recapture the thought. He felt blank, as if his memory had suddenly been wiped clean. His head was now beginning to throb with an insistent, probing pain.

Miss Venieri's eyes narrowed. 'Tell you what?'

George found it impossible to reply.

'You don't look well, Mr Zafiris.'

'No. I had an accident. I just wanted to know…' At last it

194

came to him: 'What kind of abuses you are investigating.'

She sat back, looking at him, considering something. Maybe the expression on his face, maybe his shirt. He had no idea. He saw a glass and a jug of water on the table. He reached for it.

She watched him fumble with the glass. 'You need to see a doctor,' she said.

'No,' said George. 'I'm all right.'

In an effort to prove it, he tried to pour a glass of water. The water missed the glass and splashed the table. Miss Venieri was speaking into her phone. She spoke softly but firmly. He did not hear what was said, but it sounded anxious. Anxious and soothing, and increasingly far away...

28

George woke up in a cream-coloured room with bright white neon tubes in the ceiling. His head, no longer in pain, seemed to float, without physical weight, in a halo of numbness. Sounds trickled through an open door, scrambled, unintelligible. Around him lay an orderly landscape of oxygen cylinders, trolleys, glass-fronted cabinets, stainless steel surgical instruments. He was lying on a bed, raised about a metre off the floor. The bed was on wheels.

He called out: 'Anyone there?'

The sounds from the doorway stopped. A woman in a white coat – brisk, tanned, hair tied back – approached him.

'How are you feeling?' she asked.

'Very odd.'

She nodded. 'Head? Neck?'

'Do they exist?' he said.

She smiled. 'Still there. But you've had a nasty knock.'

'Where's Sonia Venieri?'

'She had to go, but she asked me to call her when you wake up.'

'How nasty?'

'It could be worse.'

She returned through the doorway and began a new

conversation on the phone. A minute later she was back.

'Sonia will be here in ten minutes,' she said.

'Thank you, said George. 'Tell me who you are, please, and where I am.'

'I'm Dr Galini. This is my surgery.'

'Are you a friend of Sonia's?'

'Cousin.'

George repeated the word. 'Everyone is somebody's cousin,' he said, half to himself.

'How do you know Sonia?' asked the doctor.

George grunted. 'Work.'

'Are you a tax inspector?'

'No.' He smiled, amused at the thought.

'What then?'

'Private investigator.'

'Oh.' Her professional calm was suddenly ruffled. 'How does that work?'

George winced. 'It's complicated.'

'Are you investigating her, or is she investigating you?'

'It's not as simple as that. Perhaps a little of both.'

'She's the most honest person on earth. Far too honest for her own good.'

'I'm sure you're right.'

'It's typical of her to do an act of kindness even to someone who is potentially hostile.'

'Don't get the wrong idea,' said George. 'I'm not hostile.'

'But you're investigating her?'

'I've been sent by a client, who feels victimised.'

'By Sonia?'

'Correct.'

The doctor was incredulous. 'With any reason?'

'That,' said George, 'is what I'm trying to find out.'

'OK,' said the doctor. 'In other words, your client is being investigated by Sonia, and retaliates by sending you to investigate her? Accusation and counter-accusation?'

'That's roughly it.'

'Are you sure it isn't Sonia who is being victimised?'

'That's quite possible.'

'What happens if you find out that Sonia is correct and your client is wrong?'

'I shall tell the client directly.'

'Even if that's the end of the job?'

'Makes no difference. I'm an investigator, not a hoodlum.'

The doctor gave him a hard look. 'This is a disturbing story.'

'I know,' said George. 'I'm trying to do the right thing.'

The doctor continued to stare at him. 'She saved your life. You know that?'

'You said it could have been worse.'

'It could. If she hadn't brought you here, you'd probably be dying in a corridor of a public hospital.'

'So what is it? A haemorrhage?'

She nodded. 'There was some bleeding. But you're lucky. It's stopped.'

'What stopped it?'

'It stopped itself. But we had to monitor it, in case you needed surgery.'

'Did I?'

'No.'

George closed his eyes. 'Thank you,' he said.

He slept again for a while. When he woke up, he heard two women's voices in the room: Dr Galini and Sonia Venieri. He raised a hand in greeting. They were too absorbed in their conversation to notice.

'He should go home,' said the doctor. 'But he'll need care.'

'I'll take him in a taxi,' said Venieri.

George was helped to his feet.

'Can we try again with that coffee?' he asked as they emerged from the lift.

'Are you well enough?'

'God knows. We could give it a go.'

'OK.'

A bar on the opposite corner was open. They took a table.

George struggled to keep his mind clear of distracting thoughts. She was sitting between him and the light, which silhouetted her figure through the cream blouse in alarming precision of detail He out through the distraction as best he could.

'I owe you a debt of gratitude,' he said.

'We've been through that,' she replied.

'Why I'm saying it… I just want to stress that there's no hostility in what I'm doing. I just want to find out what you do and how you work.'

'On behalf of someone who is trying to stop me! I call that hostile.'

'I'm not trying to stop you doing your work. That may be my client's intention, but it's not mine.'

'So drop the case.'

'I need to do my job.'

'Your client has to be one of four or five people. What do they want to know that can possibly help them?'

'I don't know. Some weakness of yours, perhaps, some dark areas in your past, some misdemeanour, petty corruption, disloyalty, indiscretion…'

'Something to threaten me with. Blackmail me?'

'Possibly.'

'You're wasting your time. I'm a very law-abiding person.'

'We all transgress in some way.'

'Speak for yourself.'

'You don't agree? We're born sinners.'

'Rubbish.'

'You sound dangerously over-confident,' said George.

'I don't like receiving bullets in the post.'

'Has anyone offered you a *fakeláki* – a little envelope?'

'A bribe? Not yet. No doubt that will come.'

'So why don't you tell me a bit more about what you do? What sort of abuses you investigate.'

She looked exasperated. 'You don't give up, do you?'

'I just want to reach a point of understanding. I have no idea what my client might have done. If you could help me with that I could…'

'Any number of things! The basic paradigm is this. A tax inspector makes an assessment: Mr Zafiris, you owe tax of 100,000 euros. You go and protest at the tax office. The inspector says the assessment is correct. You have 20,000 euros in your pocket. This changes hands, and suddenly your tax bill is only 10,000 euros. You save thousands, the inspector gets rich, and the state continues on its wretched path of poverty and debt.'

'No trace is left? No paper trail?'

'Of the bribe no. Only the reduced tax assessment.'

'That's how you catch them?'

Her eyes flashed at him. 'I'm not going to tell you how I catch people!'

'Of course,' said George. 'That would be too easy. But I imagine you would start there.'

'Thanks for the tip. How would you go on?'

'I'd interview the people involved.'

'Who would deny everything.'

'I might resort to undercover work too.'

'Yes? What kind?'

'Send in someone with a hidden camera. Film one of these meetings where money changes hands.'

'Who?'

'I don't know. An actor, I suppose, an undercover journalist.'

'Who would have to be making a protest about a genuine tax assessment.'

'Yes. That could be tricky. The alternative is to bug the inspector's office.'

'Difficult.'

'I know someone who can do it.'

'I'm sure you do. But most of these meetings take place *outside* the office. In cafés or parks or private homes.'

'It's weird,' said George. 'Our jobs are so similar.'

'We're on opposite sides.'

'In this case, yes, but not always. In fact most of the time I'm trying to uphold the law.'

'I should stick to that if I were you.'

'Of course. If my client turns out to…'

'Another difference is that you have a mandate from an individual. Who could be anybody. A crook even.'

'I try to avoid the crooked ones.'

'Not very successfully.'

'OK,' said George. He needed to bring this to a conclusion. His head was throbbing again and he wanted to rest. 'Tell me,' he said, 'what I should say to my client.'

'I've already told you.'

'Have you?'

'Very clearly.'

'Can you tell me again?'

'Why?'

'It's gone out of my head. I'm still not feeling too good.'

'It's very simple. Tell them we are on the case. They will be caught and brought to justice. There is no escape. It's only a matter of time. If they want to minimise the damage they should come forward, give evidence, and they will be treated accordingly.'

'As scapegoats, presumably. That's what usually happens.'

'Of course not! A heavily reduced prison sentence, maybe suspended altogether. It's not a bad offer.'

'Do you expect such offers to work?'

'We do. But the bullets in the post show you what we're up against. It's a mentality. They think it's their right to be corrupt and to rob their country. One of the benefits of the job.'

George called for the bill. 'I'd better get home,' he said. 'Tomorrow I'll pass on the message to my client. Loud and clear.'

Sonia Venieri shook his hand. 'I would be most grateful,' she said. 'Thank you for making contact. In a strange way it's been useful.'

'Likewise,' said George.

'Can you get home all right?'

'I'll be fine,' said George, although he doubted it.

29

Walking to his car, George had a sense that things were not quite right. This was different from the everyday feeling that nothing quite added up – the patches of surreal wealth in a society crippled by poverty, the government drifting along like a ship with engine failure, despite the fact that there was never a Greek Prime Minister with such a strong mandate, with a big majority in Parliament and a feeble opposition lacking moral credit and leadership. It was more acute than that, more urgent, like a storm about to break. Did it come from his brain, still processing the blow to the back of his skull? Or something Miss Venieri had said? A guilty sense of attraction to her, perhaps? Or something less tangible? A sense of menace in the darkness around him?

He reached the Alfa, unlocked it, slipped softly into the driver's seat. He closed the door with a gentle click. Was anything different? Had anyone tampered with his car?

He sat still for a few moments, senses hyper-alert, observing the fall of light from the street-lamps, the shadows of the trees over pavements and roadway. He checked the mirrors. Nothing there. He lowered his window a couple of turns and listened. Everything was silent, dark and still.

Then, as if he had been expecting it, a shriek – sharp, sudden, blood-chilling. He flipped open the glove compartment and grabbed his Beretta from inside. A commotion in the gloom ahead led him on, the sounds of a car door opening, a scuffle, voices swearing. He ran towards them. A car engine started up. Its headlights snapped on. The car was manoeuvring out of a tight space. In his haste, the driver stalled. George ran up, snatching a glimpse though the back window of an arm raised to strike, another flailing to stop it. He banged on the glass. A head jerked angrily towards him, then suddenly away as the car lurched forward, tyres screeching and burning. For an instant, barely enough to be sure it happened, he caught sight of a panic-stricken woman's face.

The car was roaring away. George slipped the catch on his Beretta, aimed, pulled the trigger. He fired again, then again. One of his shots hit a tyre. The car rumbled forward, smashed into one of the line of parked cars, stopped. Two men jumped out and sprinted away. George thought of dropping them but decided against it. The priority was the woman.

He found her lying in a heap in the back seat of the car, her blouse torn, her skirt pulled up to her hips. He looked away, embarrassed at the sight, ashamed at what males are capable of.

She seemed unaware of him, so he stood a few feet away from the car and waited for her to recover. It was a minute or two before a door opened. A woman stepped cautiously out, looking up and down the street fearfully. It was Sonia. She recognised him with a start.

'Miss Venieri,' he said, 'don't be frightened.'

'What are you doing here?'

'I heard you scream. I was parked nearby.'

'Where are they?'

'They ran away.'

She blinked in confusion. 'They tried to rape me.'

'You're safe now.'

'Was that you shooting?'

'It was. Are you OK?'

She shook her head. 'Can we call the police?'

'I'll do that. Are you ready for them?'

She glanced down at her blouse; the buttons torn off, its two sides clutched together by her left hand.

'I suppose so,' she said sadly.

'Take my jacket,' he said.

Soon the street was flashing with blue lights as four young police officers arrived on motor bikes. Respectfully, carefully, they took her statement. They asked her if she knew her attackers. She said no. They inspected the car, noticed the bullet damage and the punctured tyre, but made no comment, only asking, 'Is this your car?'

'No,' she said.

The police asked George what he was doing there. He explained. They turned back to her, looked her over in silence, then stared at George again.

'Do you know each other?'

'Yes,' she said.

George nodded.

Then, to George: 'Are you armed?'

George said, 'Yes,' and raised his arms. 'You can check my weapon. In my trouser pocket. It's licensed.'

A policeman reached his hand into George's pocket, coming out with the Beretta. Unspoken questions hovered in the air.

'I'll need to take this,' said the policeman in charge.

'I'd like a receipt,' said George. 'That's an expensive weapon.'

'I know.'

The police sent a request by radio for the car to be towed away. Two of the officers set off, two remained. The one in charge said, 'We have to wait for the tow truck. You two can go.'

George offered Sonia a lift home, which she refused. He did not insist. Instead he called for a taxi and told the driver to make sure she got safely into her house. He gave his number to both the driver and her.

'Be vigilant,' he told her. 'If you see anything suspicious when you get home, don't go in. Call me at once.'

'You don't think they could be there?'

'It's possible.'

She stopped to think.

'Would you mind accompanying me?'

'Of course not. That's why I offered you a lift.'

'We'll go by taxi. The driver can wait while you see me in, then he can bring you back here.'

'That's fine.'

He could see what she was doing. Sensible.

She lived in Maroussi, in a small modern building near the Town Hall. Four apartments, all glass and concrete, like four brightly-lit stages in a stack. Not the most discreet of homes.

'You have window blinds, I hope?' said George.

'I do. Come up quickly than I'll let you go.'

George followed her up the stairs to her apartment. He waited in the entrance as she checked the rooms, switching on lights as she went. Within a minute she was back.

'All clear.' Then, with a suddenly exhausted look, 'What a strange afternoon.'

'For the record,' George said, 'I don't think my client sent those two bastards, but if she did...'

'She?'

George stopped.

'You said "she".'

George said, 'The taxi's waiting.'

'Forget the taxi. Your client is Mrs Katramis.'

'I can't tell you that,' said George.

'There's only one woman I'm investigating, so it must be her.'

'I'm not confirming or denying,' said George, feeling stupider than he had felt for a very long time.

'At last you've told me something useful,' she said.

'Be careful,' said George.

She nodded coldly and saw him out of the door.

30

After a long, heavy, troubled sleep, George opened his eyes to a bright morning, the sun's beams slanting through the open bedroom door. He followed their track to the kitchen and saw a note on the table.

Gone out for the day. Hope your head is better.

Disappointed that his wife had not bothered to stay and check that he was all right, he padded round the kitchen like a melancholy bear. Feeling too lazy to make his daily Greek coffee, his sacred *kafedáki,* he took a tin of instant coffee from the cupboard, tossed a spoonful into a cup and mixed it with boiling water. After one sip he pulled a face and added milk, after a second he tried adding some sugar, after a third he gave up and poured the whole lot down the drain. It was unspeakably foul. He started again the proper way: fresh coffee, sugar, water, stirred together in the *briki* over a sharp flame, and left to bubble and rise. It never failed, just as the instant coffee never really succeeded.

While waiting for the coffee to boil he foraged for something to eat. He found a rice pudding in the fridge, a slab of cheese, a few slices of bread. All left over from Nick's visit. Since then neither George nor Zoe had been shopping or thought very much about food. It was, he reflected, symbolic of their superannuated life as a couple. The family as a place of warmth, conviviality and love – where had that gone? It existed only as long as their child was with them.

The coffee rose in the pot. George switched off the gas at the exact moment when the foam touched the brim – a delicate piece of timing, long practised, never free of anxious excitement as the residual heat kept the froth rising for a few seconds and threatening to spill over. At the critical moment the thrust of it would fade, dying from within. He knew it would, it had to, yet it always seemed surprising, as if he'd got away with something.

He poured the coffee into a cup, set it down on the table, and waited for it to cool.

His phone rang. Haris was on the line, as vibrantly energetic as ever.

'Haris, what can I do for you?'

'Get me a cup of coffee. A double preferably.'

'Where are you?'

'Down in the street.'

'I've just made one. There's enough for you. Come up.'

Haris bounded in like a dog excited to see its master.

'What's up?' asked George, pushing the cup across the table.

Haris took a sip, rolled his eyes in appreciation and clapped his hands.

'Last night,' he said, 'I heard an incredible conversation. Leonidas Papaspirou, Olli's father, discussing with his wife the marriage prospects of their daughter.'

'I thought they were totally clear.'

'We all did.'

'But…'

'Mr Papaspirou is worried about Olli's fiancé.'

'He heard about the bugging?'

'More serious than that. The Katramis business is in difficulties.'

George was astonished. Haris gave him a pat on the shoulder. 'I know. It's hard to believe.'

Finding his voice at last, George said, 'How the hell does Papaspirou know?'

'He's a nerd! Spends every waking hour on financial research.'

'What kind of difficulties? Did he say?'

'They're borrowing too much.' Haris smiled ruefully. 'The national vice.'

'Does he want Olli to break off the engagement?'

'That's the general idea.'

'Hell, he must be serious.'

'It could be an excuse.'

'What do you mean?'

'He doesn't like Pandelís.'

'Are you sure about that?'

'I've heard him say it.'

'Does he like anybody?'

Haris smiled brightly. 'He likes me!'

'OK, Haris, but you're not trying to marry his daughter. What does Mrs Papaspirou say?'

'She just panicked. What will people say? The shame! *Rezili!* Flapping about like a butterfly on cocaine.'

'She wants to go on with the wedding?'

Haris flung up his hands. 'No one knows what she wants. Least of all herself.'

George sipped his coffee. He was feeling hungry.

'Do you want to eat something?' he asked.

'Always.'

'There isn't much in the fridge. I can probably manage a toasted cheese sandwich.'

'Perfect.'

George opened the fridge and got busy.

Haris said, 'I really came round to discuss the Lazaridis raid.'

'How's it looking?'

'We had a recce yesterday. Third floor office, five rooms, two looking onto the street. Concierge on the ground floor, access by lift and stairs. The door to the office is sealed, but only with yellow and black parcel tape and an official letter.'

'Is there a guard?'

'No.'

'Surveillance cameras?'

'No.'

'That's sloppy. What's to stop us going in?'

'The concierge and the official letter.'

'Which says what?'

'According to law number five million seven hundred and eighty four thousand two hundred and sixty three, paragraph 748B, this office is under seal by government mandate and anyone attempting to enter will be prosecuted.'

'Does it frighten you?'

'Not in the least.'

'So what's the plan?'

'We'll use a furniture removal to distract the concierge, then open up so you can go in.'

'Just me?'

'You know what you're looking for.'

George was doubtful.

'You do know what you're looking for,' said Haris, 'don't you?'

'I've got a general idea.'

'That's more than the rest of us.'

'How long will I have?'

'Fifteen minutes.'

'Jeez, that's tight. How do you get through the files of an entire lawyer's office in fifteen minutes?'

'I'm sure Mr Zamir will train you.'

They ate the toasted sandwiches and had another cup of coffee, and then George asked Haris to take a look at the back of his head. Haris stood up, walked round the back of George's chair, and fired off an expletive. 'What happened here?'

George gave a brief account of his visit to Marathon.

Haris groaned. 'You shouldn't go into these risky situations on your own. That was damn stupid. I've told you before.'

'I didn't know it was risky.'

'If you'd thought about it you'd have known. A Pakistani was killed out there.'

'I'm not a Pakistani.'

'Oh for heaven's sake!'

'OK,' said George, 'I behaved naïvely. And I paid the price.'

'Are you going back there?'

'Only with reinforcements.'

'What's your plan?'

'I don't know. If I go after Sebastian Yerakas I could miss the father, who's the real crook. If I try to nail the father, I could be in for a very long battle.'

'In what sense is he the real crook? The son's running the farm, he's responsible, no?'

'You should have seen him on the phone to his father. No backbone. Just a feeble little flare of resistance, then "Yes, Daddy, anything you say".'

'So you need more proof of the father's guilt? How will you get that?'

'I'm thinking about it.'

31

Colonel Sotiriou had the harassed air of a general on a far-flung campaign. His office was being redecorated, dust sheets shrouding the great stacks of documents which had been crammed together in half the room to give the painters space to work. The scratching of sandpaper on plaster and a steady downpour of dust accompanied the conversation he was conducting on the telephone.

'Stop talking, you ass, and listen! Check the name, address, date of purchase, make, model and colour of car, licence plate. Every last detail! Call the Ministry of Transport, get the latest updates. I want no mistakes! No approximations. No assumptions. Only facts! Understood? Facts! Now: repeat my instructions. I said, *repeat my instructions!*'

He waved George towards the only free chair in the room while he listened impatiently to his subordinate's reply.

'All right,' he said with quiet menace. 'Go and do all that now. I want results in 15 minutes... I know that's tight, it's *deliberately* tight! So get moving!'

He put down the phone, pulled an exasperated face, and reached his hand across the desk in greeting.

'When you work with careless people you get horrible

results,' he said. 'I'm not referring to the painters, who do an excellent job. I wish they were on my staff... Do you know, incidentally, what percentage of cases the public prosecutor wins in court?'

'No.'

'Have a guess!'

'Sixty?'

'No!'

'Fifty?'

The Colonel pointed downwards.

'Forty?'

'Less!'

'Twenty?'

'Even less!'

'Ten?'

'Exactly! Isn't that appalling?'

'Why so few?'

'Evidence poorly collected, ignorance of criminal law, a general antipathy to precision and accuracy. And our old friend "take it easy"!'

'You're talking about your fellow police officers?'

'Who else?'

'Don't you train them?'

'Of course we train them! But we're fighting an entire culture: sloth, laziness, indifference, incompetence, the whole Levantine catastrophe. It's a lonely battle. A desperate battle! And we're losing it.'

'So what's this latest thing?'

Sotiriou's face went blank. 'What latest thing?'

'That phone call. The Ministry of Transport?'

'I can't tell you.'

'You never can.'

'As you know, Zafiris, I can't speak about my work. But you can speak about yours. Why are you here?'

'I want to report two violent incidents.'

'You can do that at the duty desk.'

'After what you've just told me?'

'No no, they're fine over there.'

'I want to see *you*.'

'But did you ask if I want to see you?'

'You never want to see me.'

'That's true. You bring trouble.'

'And you have enough of your own.'

'Precisely!'

'So why do you add to your problems by having the decorators in?'

'It's not my decision.'

'But you don't move out?'

'Never!'

'Why?'

'I like to keep an eye on my collection.'

'You think they'll damage something?'

'No, they're very careful.'

'Which contradicts your theory about lazy Levantines.'

'Don't try and be clever with me, Zafiris! This redecoration is utterly unnecessary. It was last done five years ago and the paintwork is still unblemished. We are supposed to be short of money! This is a political job. I'm getting close to some sensitive material. To the rotten heart of this suffering state. If I move out, the protectors of corruption will move in, they

will search through my files like a pack of sniffer dogs to find
what evidence I have uncovered in my investigations, and then
they will destroy it. But I'm onto them! Everything sensitive is
backed up. And I'm not budging from this spot!'

'Do you sleep in here too?'

'Don't be stupid. I go home at night.'

'So then the office is unguarded.'

'No. I have a personal lock on the door. When I have to go
out in the day, I go. And my friends Christoforos and Harilaos,
the painters, go too. I'm careful, Zafiris! Now, tell me, what do
you want? Make it snappy.'

'I was assaulted yesterday out at Marathon.'

'Seriously?'

'Very. A blow to the back of the head.'

'Motive?'

'I'm not sure. Perhaps because I was asking questions
about our Pakistani friend.'

'Any idea who did it?'

'Yes. A very good idea.'

'Fine. Give all the details to the duty sergeant. Next?'

'Wait. I'll do all that, but this needs a careful touch. I was
there with Sebastian, son of Simeon Yerakas.'

'Really?'

'The man who hit me is the supervisor on the Yerakas
estate. He's a roughneck, employed by the old man. Very
cocky, pushes the son around in the name of the father. I think
he employs the Pakistanis directly. He may well have killed
Wasim.'

'His name?'

'I don't know.'

218

'How do we find him?'

'I can go with you.'

'We'll arrange that. What about your second case?'

'Hang on. The point is, to be clear about responsibility. This brute is employed by Yerakas.'

'I know.'

'The father, not the son.'

'I've got that!'

'If you arrest the son...'

'Relax. We won't arrest him. Or the father.'

'What about the supervisor?'

'We can arrest him. Next case?'

'This concerns a Miss Sonia Venieri.'

Sotiriou was taken aback. He tried at once to hide his reaction, but not soon enough.

'You know her?' asked George, surprised.

'I do.'

'I'm sorry to say she suffered an attempted rape last night.'

Sotiriou's look darkened. 'Tell me...'

George described the events he had witnessed. The Colonel listened carefully.

'Did you get the registration number of the car?'

'I did.' George read it from his notebook.

The Colonel nodded, but said nothing more.

'I suppose it's too much to ask how you know her?'

'It is,' said the Colonel.

'Has she reported the crime?'

The Colonel hesitated. Instead of replying, he asked, 'What is your connection with her – if any?'

'My car was parked nearby.'

The Colonel eyed him suspiciously. 'There is some information missing,' he said. 'You know her name. You have some connection with her, I'm sure of it.'

George said nothing. He enjoyed playing the Colonel at his own game . But it was possible that the Colonel knew more than he was letting on.

'I don't know how you can be sure of what must simply be a suspicion,' George said.

The Colonel continued to stare at him sceptically.

'Stop playing games, Zafiris. I can smell information! Particularly *unspoken* information! You know more. And this was a serious crime.'

'So let's stick to the crime, shall we? Not irrelevant personal questions?'

'You are becoming defensive. An inevitable sign!'

'And you are becoming aggressive. Also an inevitable sign.'

'Of what?'

'Of me being about to walk out.'

'All right,' said Sotiriou. 'Let's just say that I'm aware of the case.'

'I suspected as much,' said George.

'What do you know?'

'I don't understand your question.'

'About Sonia Venieri.'

'I know that she's a tax inspector.'

'An ordinary tax inspector?'

'An auditor.'

'Correct. She inspects the inspectors.' The Colonel paused, waiting for a reaction. George said nothing.

'Among the inspectors under her scrutiny,' Sotiriou went on, 'is a certain senior inspector, a woman, whom I believe you know.'

George met the Colonel's stony gaze with one of his own.

'Is that what she told you?'

'Do you deny it?'

'I neither confirm nor deny it.'

'Why not just admit it?'

'Because, Colonel, I have rules of confidentiality too!'

'Fine. I'll take that as a yes.'

'Take it any way you like.'

The Colonel went on calmly. 'You would be well advised, Zafiris, to stop playing cat and mouse with me.'

'It's the only game you seem to know.'

'No, Zafiris.' The Colonel became solemn. 'I know other games too. Chess, for example, in which the purpose of a move may only be revealed several moves later.'

George nodded and said lightly, 'Any others?'

'Yes,' said the Colonel. 'Tennis. Which I believe you like to play too.' He paused. 'The ball, as they say, is in your court.'

George felt as if an icy hand had touched his back. He had used exactly that phrase to Sonia Venieri. Either this was a coincidence of the most bizarre kind, or Colonel Sotiriou had somehow been privy to that conversation.

'We can play tennis if you prefer,' said George.

'Willingly. But it takes two to play.'

That was beyond coincidence.

'You obviously know Miss Venieri very well,' said George. 'Is she related to you? A friend? A lover even?'

'She is a colleague,' said Sotiriou stiffly.

'She obviously tells you a great deal about her life.'

The Colonel picked up a pencil and examined the point with a critical eye.

'Where do you think this conversation is going?' he asked.

'I wish I knew,' said George. 'I've told you about the two incidents. One you evidently know about already. The other I hope you will act on. Apart from that I've finished.'

'Right! I shall let you know when we can send a squad to Marathon to bring in the man you describe as "the supervisor". Your help may be needed to identify him.' He paused, tilting the pencil up and down between his fingers. 'Meanwhile, I suggest you go and see the tax inspector that I mentioned – the senior tax inspector – and tell her to behave more correctly.'

'What's that supposed to mean?'

'She will know.'

'And you expect her to listen?'

'Frankly, no.'

'What's the point in telling her?'

'We always hope,' said the Colonel, 'that one of these parasites, these troglodytes, will experience a flash of insight, a spark of awareness, that will illuminate, for an instant, the perpetual night in which they live. It's a lot to ask, and 99% are utterly incapable of it. Unfortunately it seems we must break in from the outside. Only then do they understand. When it's too late to save themselves.'

'You're speaking in riddles.'

The Colonel ignored him. He was talking as if to himself. 'The light of understanding dawns at different times to different people. For one, in the parliamentary elections. For another, when the doorbell rings at five in the morning. But it will come. It will come inevitably. Night must fall, they say, but the sun also rises!'

George wondered what all this was about.

There was a knock on the door. The Colonel started, as if from a dream. 'Come in!'

A young officer entered. 'We've had the confirmation, sir.'

'Yes?'

'The car is registered to Mrs Katramis.'

'That's definite, is it?'

'100%, sir.'

'Thank you.'

'Anything else, sir? Any follow-up action?'

'Not for now. I'll give the signal.'

'Thank you sir.' The young man retreated.

Before he was fully out of the room, the Colonel called him back. 'Someone shot out the tyres,' he said. 'Do we have an ID on the weapon used?'

'No, sir. We know it was a Beretta Jet Fire, but we haven't traced the owner yet.'

'Let me know just as soon as you have a result.'

This time he let the young man go. As the door closed, he turned back to George. 'There you are,' he said. 'The time bomb is ticking.'

32

Maria's phone rang and rang. At last it switched to the answering service: *Due to exceptional pressure of work I cannot take your call. Leave a message or try later.*

George was on his way to her office but left a message anyway. 'I need to see you,' he said. 'Please call me at once.'

Ten minutes later she rang back. 'I'm busy, Yiorgo *mou.* What's this about?'

'We need to talk. Urgently.'

'That's impossible. I'm in a meeting.'

'End it.'

'I can't. I'm with a government minister.'

'End it, I tell you. Or the police will.'

'What do they want?'

'They want to know why two men tried to rape a certain tax auditor in a car that belongs to you.'

'Mother of Christ! How did… Where are you?'

'On my way over.'

'All right. I'll find a way to see you. Just for a couple of minutes.'

At the tax building he zigzagged through the crowds in the lobby to the stairs at the back. He climbed to the second floor. Outside the door marked *Deputy Chief Inspector of Taxes* he paused for a moment, preparing himself for the unpleasantness ahead. He knocked and walked in. A secretary looked up at him indifferently from behind his desk.

'Tell Mrs Katramis Mr Zafiris is here.'

The secretary eyed him arrogantly.

'She's waiting for me.'

Pursing his lips disdainfully, taking his time, the secretary picked up the phone.

A minute later another door opened and Maria Katramis appeared. With her were two men, evidently rich. George recognised them both. One was Byron Kakridis, Minister of Development: tall, black-bearded, with long slicked-back hair, more like a rock and roll promoter than a politician. The other was Simeon Yerakas, the silky-smooth manipulator of people and events. Neither of them recognised George. Neither was in a good mood.

Maria said, 'Please, gentlemen, give me five minutes with my cousin. That's all I ask. It's an emergency. When it's family, as you know, we have to respond to those in need… Please, take a seat.'

Kakridis and Yerakas came in and sat down, stony-faced.

'We're waiting,' said Kakridis.

George followed Maria into her office. As soon as the door was shut she said angrily, 'I have never done a thing like that before! If this isn't important I'm going to kill you.'

'Maria, you have five minutes to make the most important decision of your life.'

'Oh yes? What's that?'

'Either you come clean with the Venieri woman and the police or you will be arrested.'

'Arrested? For what exactly?'

'Attempted kidnapping and rape, as well as whatever sharp practices have been going on in this office.'

'That's ridiculous!'

'Your car?'

'It was stolen.'

'Did you report it?'

'I didn't know it had gone.'

'You think those two thugs are going to take the rap for you?'

'Which two thugs?'

'Oh come on! You're willing to risk everything? On a lie?'

'You don't understand, Yiorgo.'

'No, *you* don't understand, Maria. The only way to save yourself now is to co-operate…'

'Don't give me that bullshit!'

'…with the investigation.'

'There is not going to be an investigation!'

'That's not what I heard.'

'Who do you talk to? Because I talk to the Minister!'

'He's under investigation too!'

This was a fantasy, but worth a try.

She shook her head. 'Things don't work like that at this level, Yiorgo. I understand your alarm, but I can handle the situation. You'd better go now so that I can…'

'Carry on dealing with crooks like Yerakas and Kakridis, destroying our economy, poisoning our democracy?'

'Don't talk like that! They are top flight individuals!'

'I know them both, Maria. They're unscrupulous, vicious men.'

'You've been listening to lies, Yiorgo. One day I will explain the truth to you, but not now. Go! I don't have any more time.'

'What are those two "top flight individuals" doing here?'

'You're overdoing it now!'

'All right, Maria, I've given you your chance. You're on your own now.'

As he turned to leave she gripped his arm. 'That little snake has bitten you,' she hissed.

'Sorry?'

'Some maniac started shooting at the car last night. Who was that? Who's protecting her? And why?'

George said nothing.

'These people don't know what harm they do,' she went on. 'You've met her, haven't you? Sanctimonious little shit!'

'Maria, I'm telling you for the last time. It's not just Venieri. It's the police too. They're onto you and all your Ottoman practices here in the tax office.'

'Get out, Yiorgo. Let's talk politics another day.'

'That will be too late.'

'I'll take my chances.'

She moved quickly for the door and opened it, saying in a public voice, 'Thank you, cousin, for your visit. You did well to come when you did. I hope my dear aunt survives the operation. Please give her all my love.'

The two VIPs stood up without a word and walked past him into Maria's office.

George climbed the stairs to the third floor. He wanted to see Sonia Venieri. It was an instinctive urge. His brief conversation with Maria Katramis had disturbed him.

He knocked on the door. An irritable 'Who is it?' prompted him in. Sonia Venieri sat at a desk straight in front of him, her hair pulled tight in a harsh ponytail, dark glasses covering her eyes. She radiated hostile fragility.

'Oh,' she said coldly. 'It's you.'

'Am I disturbing you?'

'To tell you the truth, yes.'

'OK, I'll go.'

'What do you want?'

'To see how you are.'

'I'm all right.'

'Really?'

She lifted her dark glasses from puffy, red, exhausted eyes.

'How the hell *could* I be all right?'

'Anything I can do?'

'You have to be joking!'

'I'm sorry.'

The dark glasses went on again.

'Nothing, thank you. I just have to get through this.'

'That's the right approach,' said George.

Receiving no answer, he glanced around the room. There were two framed newspapers on the wall above her desk. One from the day after the last general election, announcing the victory of Alexis Tsipras and his Syriza party, and one from the referendum called by Tsipras in 2015.

'Are you a supporter?' he asked.

'I was,' she said. 'When I thought they stood for something.'

'You've changed your mind?'

She gave him a look of incredulity mixed with contempt. 'Hasn't everyone?'

'Why do you keep those up there on the wall?'

'As a reminder.'

'Of what?'

'Don't torment me,' she said. 'The dream was sweet while it lasted.'

He watched her sad face for a moment or two. 'I've just spoken to Maria Katramis,' he said.

'Lucky man!'

'You know she's my wife's cousin?'

'That might explain a few things.'

'Such as?'

'I don't know. Your defence of her awful behaviour, perhaps. I'll bear it in mind.'

'I've also seen Colonel Sotiriou.'

'Ah.' She smiled a small, tight, secret smile. 'Uncle Costa.'

'Uncle Costa? Is that his nickname in the tax office?'

'No. He's my uncle. My mother is his sister.'

'Are you close?'

She nodded.

'See him often?'

'Sunday lunch every week for as long as I can remember.'

'*That* might explain a few things.'

'You know him well?' she asked.

'Through my work. Obviously he has a personal life which I'm not part of. Except he did tell me once that he writes haiku in Linear B. Extraordinary.'

'You've seen him today?'

'I have.'

He wondered how much to say. 'You and he speak the same language.'

'I like to think so.'

'He wants Maria Katramis to give evidence.'

'Of course.'

'I've just tried to persuade her.'

'And?'

'Hopeless.'

'She's an arrogant woman.'

'She had two big shots with her just now. What she called "top flight individuals".'

'Who?'

'Simeon Yerakas was one.'

'Of course.'

'Why "of course"?'

'They're like this.' She linked her two little fingers. 'And the other?'

'Byron Kakridis.'

'The Minister?' She looked surprised.

'The same.'

'That *is* news.'

'I know,' said George, 'that Kakridis and Yerakas are very close.'

'Are they related?'

'Somehow. I forget how. But their business interests interlock. The legislator, the property developer. Kakridis opens the road politically, and Yerakas exploits it. And so they both get richer.'

'Why not the tax inspector too? And her husband the builder?'

'She feels invulnerable,' said George. 'Perhaps because of those two.'

'And others like them.'

'I just wonder,' said George, 'do you have any chance against interests like that?'

Venieri frowned. 'Against Kakridis none at all. As a member of Parliament he's immune from prosecution. Against Yerakas very little. He's extremely powerful. My only chance is against Katramis.'

'Isn't she powerful too?'

'Let's see.'

'You seem determined,' said George. 'And you need to be.'

She shrugged this off. 'It's my job.'

Her desk telephone rang. 'Excuse me.'

George watched her take the call. Her face, at first puzzled, became bewildered and then angry.

'Who decided this? When? I haven't finished yet! How can it be more urgent?' She slammed down the phone.

'Bastards! Shameless bastards!'

'What's happened?'

She shook her head, overcome with violent emotion. 'I can't tell you. I can't tell you anything. You'd better go now.'

'I'm going,' said George.

33

Home, George had always believed, should be a happy place, where food, rest, affection and the comfort of familiar things could act on the suffering soul, restoring strength and hope. Since Zoe's discovery of her inner Fury, however, the flat on Aristotle Street had become a place of torment. George dreaded going home. He waved a weary hello to Dimitri at the Café Agamemnon, turned the key in the street door, and climbed the stairs with heavy limbs and horrible misgivings in his heart.

Zoe was waiting for him. She wasted no time in firing off a first salvo.

'Have you spoken to Nick?' she asked.

'Not today.'

'You should have.'

'Oh?'

'He's taken a job with Musk.'

'Elon Musk? The American?'

'No! That bloody Scandinavian transport company.'

'Maersk.'

'*Maerrrrrsssskkk!* What a name! It sounds like a Swedish version of *merde!*'

'They're a major company. That's a big step forward for him.'

She pulled a sour face. 'He says he's discussed it with you, and you approve.'

'Absolutely!'

'Despite *everything* we said?'

George kept calm. 'It was Nick's choice.'

'You should be *guiding* him as a father.'

'Guiding or dictating?'

'What difference does it make? He's throwing away a golden opportunity here in Athens, and you're just watching him do it with a goddam smile on your face!'

'You've got this wrong, Zoe.'

'Oh yes? Are you not smiling? Blessing his stupidity?'

'It's not a stupid decision.'

'What the hell do you know? When did you ever make anything *but* a stupid decision?'

George said, 'I'm not prepared to discuss matters like this, Zoe. All shouting and insults.'

'It's the only way to get through to you.'

'I stop listening as soon as you start ranting like this. If you want to talk about Nick…'

'If *I* want to? And you don't? Our son?!'

'Of course I want to. But not like this.'

'How then?'

'Have you forgotten what a proper conversation sounds like? Where each respects the other's opinion, considers it with an open mind…'

'Oh bullshit! The only opinion you ever consider is your own!'

233

'That's much more true of you than me.'

'Oh don't be so fucking patronising!'

George put down his briefcase. 'Zoe, come on, let's not fight.'

'You leave me no choice.'

'OK, you want to fight. I don't. So I'm not going to say anything. I'm going to get a beer and you can talk as much as you like.'

George opened the fridge, reached for a beer, and noticed a packet of pills on the shelf. A glance at the label told him it was the anti-depressant she had been taking a couple of years ago, the one with all the side-effects. Still, he reflected, even that long list of horrors didn't include raging at your loved ones.

He returned to the sitting room, opened the beer, and slumped down exhaustedly into an armchair. He took a slug from the can, felt the fizz on his tongue, the icy liquid down his throat, and said, 'Shoot.'

Zoe let him have it with both barrels. What a mess he had made of his life, what a wretched example he had been to his own son. Patiently he listened, mentally deflecting the blast of her anger onto an imaginary Other George, an unfortunate figure who might fit the description of moral, psychological and financial delinquency that she was so mercilessly developing. When she had finished, or at any rate stopped to take a breather, he asked, 'Are you sure the Katramis offer is still there?'

'Of course it is!' she cried. 'Why would it not be?'

'Because they're in trouble.'

'What do you mean?'

'Financial trouble.'

'Nonsense!'

'It's true.'

'Who told you?'

'Someone who knows, who studies these things.'

'One of your leftwing university friends, no doubt! Spreading false rumours to discredit the creators of wealth.'

'Not so.'

'Who then?'

'I'm not saying.'

'I don't believe you.'

'OK, don't. But I'm telling you: quite apart from the reasons I've given why Maersk is a million times better bet for Nick, we now have the genuine prospect of Katramis going bust.'

'Show me the evidence.'

'I can't. But the news comes from a reliable source, an expert investor, and I have no doubt it will be confirmed very soon.'

George watched his words take effect. Zoe's rage faltered, uncertain, then quickly turned another way, seeking a new path of attack.

'What I find hurtful,' she said, 'is that you talk to Nick behind my back, ignoring my advice, ignoring my family, in fact insulting them with your disrespect. Treating us as if we barely exist! But just wait until Maersk hits hard times. See how loyal *they* turn out to be!'

'That's a risk, I admit. A small one, but still a risk. I trust Nick to do well, though, and make himself a valued member of the company.'

'But why for a bunch of Scandinavians and not his own family?'

'His own family operates in an antiquated business culture, riddled with corruption and moral hazard. It's doomed.'

'Oh, "doomed" is it? As doomed as you?'

George said nothing.

'And with your advice,' she went on, hotting up again, 'you can say good bye to your son! Because he will be off working in Oslo or Jakarta and we'll never see him!'

'That's the least of my worries. He must find fulfilment in his work. In a decent company that respects the law, pays its taxes, contributes to society, and challenges its young employees by giving them responsibility. Not boring them into submission for thirty years like the Greeks do!'

'You have no idea what you're talking about!'

George felt his own anger rising now.

'Why don't you stop wasting your time with me then? Get out and leave me to my ideas, and let's see who turns out to be right.'

'By then the damage will be done!'

'So what do you suggest?'

'Call Nick and order him – *order him,* I say! – to take the job with Stelios and Maria!'

'That would be folly. I wouldn't dream of inflicting such a fate on my son.'

'You know what? You're a bastard as well as an asshole!'

'Thank you,' said George. 'It's good to be appreciated.'

Zoe stood up, grabbed her bag, and marched out, slamming the front door.

Down at the Café Agamemnon, as the lights came on, George asked Dimitri to bring him a beer and call the local taverna for a plate of roast chicken, red peppers and potatoes.

'No food at home tonight, Mr George?'

'No food, Dimitri. And no company.'

'I can give you both. If you're in the mood, of course.'

'With you, Dimitri, always.'

'You're too kind. It's getting harder every day to find anyone worth talking to.'

'Why is that?'

'Who knows? People don't seem to be as well educated. Also I think they've forgotten how to talk, unless it's on their phones. And what do they say on the phone? "OK." "Cool". "See you at 8." Whereas you, Mr George, you're old school. The art of conversation has a meaning for you.'

George laughed. 'What's on your mind, Dimitri? This sounds like the prelude to some grand pronouncement.'

'I'll tell you. We've just heard from Mr Tsakalotos, our very wealthy, privately educated, Marxist, and in my view mentally unbalanced Minister of Finance. He says our country has *come through the worst of the crisis*, and we no longer need bailouts.'

'Do you believe him?'

'No!'

'Neither do I.'

'Good! But *why* don't you believe him?'

'Basic economics. The debt hasn't been paid off. We have simply borrowed more to pay the interest on the original loan. So the debt has increased.'

'Exactly. Just tell me, Mr George, if I've got this right. In 2009, at the start of this crisis, out national debt was 300 billion euros. Now it's 319 billion. And we're not paying it off

237

because our annual budget is in permanent deficit too. Each year the problem's getting worse, not better! How come we no longer need help?'

'You're right. It's nonsense.'

'You and I are the only ones who realise this?'

'Anyone with the most elementary grasp of figures can work it out.'

'Right. So how does this charlatan – and the rest of those fantasists in government – get away with lying like this?'

'That's a good question,' said George. 'My own theory is that the truth is too painful to bear. So we prefer a lie. A comfortable lie.'

'You really think we are so childish?'

'I see no other explanation.'

'Don't you think the Greek people are fed up?'

'Of course! That's why Tsakalotos is offering them this fairytale.'

'I don't mean fed up with austerity! I mean fed up with the way Greece has been run the last decades.'

'That too. But this government claims to be different. Rather than see that claim for what it is – a myth – people prefer to live in hope of change.'

'Even if they know it's a lie?'

'We don't know if they understand that or not. As long as 40 percent of the electorate prefers myths to reality, Mr Tsakalotos and his friends will stay in power. Politics isn't really about ideas, you know. It's about numbers.'

Dimitri was aghast. 'How can you say that? And so calmly? This is a national tragedy!'

'I'm ashamed to be calm, Dimitri, believe me. I admire your

agitation. But nothing we say or do will change it! Politicians are professional power hunters. They work at a level beyond our reach, crafting slogans and ideas in a space of their own where the connections with reality are minimal. Their advisors are public relations specialists, pollsters and psephologists. We are to them what wood is to a carpenter. We are powerless, except for a periodic chance to vote for a new set of promises.'

'Then what is democracy?'

'A great idea, perverted.'

'Don't say that! I'll shoot myself.'

'No, Dimitri! Please don't do that! Or if you do, kindly bring me that beer first…'

'Oh! I forgot. At once, Mr George.'

Dimitri hurried to the bar.

The food arrived, and George ate hungrily. He was upset about Zoe, but deeply annoyed by her unquestioning obsession with the family. No compromise was possible over that. Nick had made his decision. She was wrong to attack him over that and she must at some point realise it. Meanwhile she would undoubtedly carry on shouting and insulting him until her anger was exhausted or he left her in exasperation. In which case she could scream it all out on her own.

He considered the wider situation. The Katramis drama was playing out according to its own twisted logic. Maria had refused his advice. That was her problem. Her husband's construction business was possibly going down, and there was nothing George could do to affect that. Their son Pandelís would either marry Olli or find some other victim of his controlling personality. Olli now had a chance to break free, and it was up to her if she took it. He hoped she had the guts to do the right thing, but he had his doubts. Sonia Venieri was in the middle of some horrible work crisis but that, he told himself, was probably a daily occurrence.

The remaining conundrum was Yerakas, father and son, and that poor smashed-up Pakistani, Wasim. There was also the murdered lawyer Lazaridis. A weird thought came to him, born in the randomness of the moment. Was there some connection between them?

34

The call came later that evening. George was at home, thinking about going to bed, wondering if Zoe would return. He had just sent her a text message saying *Where are you? I don't want to fight*, when his phone rang.

'Mr Zafiris, this is Flamur Zamir. We will be at the Lazaridis office at 10.45 tomorrow morning. We are expecting you. Be there a few minutes early, please. My boys will make a distraction for the concierge. There will be shouting, maybe a little rough stuff, nothing serious. Ignore it. Go to the third floor. The door will be open for you. Don't forget to bring a suitcase for documents.'

'Haris told me I would have just fifteen minutes in there.'

'Correct.'

'That's not long enough.'

'It's plenty.'

'It's a lawyer's office, Mr Zamir, not a private apartment.'

'No different!'

'He said you would give me a lesson in how to...'

'No lesson is needed. You will work fast. Adrenalin handles everything.'

'Adrenalin won't open a locked filing cabinet. Or a safe.'

'I will be there. I have all the instruments.'

'What about the escape plan? Is that clear?'

'Your friend Haris has fixed it all. He is very thorough. Any more questions?… OK. Then I will see you in the morning.'

As he ended the call he saw a reply had come from Zoe. *Staying with a friend. Speak tomorrow. Z*

The next morning at ten, George loaded an empty suitcase into the boot of a taxi and told the driver to go to Valaoritou Street. This was just round the corner from the Lazaridis office in Amerikis. It was not a long way to Valaoritou Street, but the traffic turned out to be unusually bad. It gave the driver all the scope he needed to rant freely about politics, philosophy, and the physical and moral state of the universe.

Only half listening, George checked his watch anxiously as 1030 approached and passed. Three blocks away he decided to walk, paid the driver, and hurried along on foot past the line of honking cars in Panepistimiou. He found the corner of Amerikis obstructed by an enormous articulated truck that had taken the corner too sharply and was now jammed across the entrance to the street, causing a long, angry tailback. In Amerikis itself, up at the far end, a smaller truck was blocking the road, hazard lights flashing, rear shutter raised. Two delivery men were wrestling an enormous pale green sofa down onto the pavement. As George approached, the men rang the bell at Number 23. A heavily built man in his fifties emerged, pale, grey, balding, in a dirty blue jogging suit. This must be the concierge. The delivery man at the front end of the sofa rested his load and took a piece of paper from his pocket. The concierge pointed to the suite of bell pushes in the doorway. The delivery man pointed to the piece of paper. The concierge pointed again at the bells. An argument developed. Hands flew, voices rose. As the anger mounted, Flamur Zamir and Haris strolled out from a neighbouring doorway and into the building. George walked slowly up the pavement, heard the concierge tell the men they were fools. One of the delivery men said, 'I have to deliver this sofa to this address today! Otherwise I don't get paid. So open up, buster, or get out of the way.'

'Nobody ordered a sofa!'

'Yes they did! It's here on the delivery note.'

'They did not!'

'What do you call this? A pork chop?'

'If a delivery's expected, I'm the first one to know. No one told me, so there's no delivery. Take it away.'

'No sir! This sofa is coming to this address. You better call Mr Whoever it is that ordered it and tell him.'

'That's your job.'

George slipped in through the open door behind the concierge's back, across the hall and up the shadowy staircase to the third floor. Haris was waiting on the landing. He nodded towards an open door. 'Zamir's in there,' he said. 'Close the door behind you.'

Cautiously George entered the office. He was struck by a stale smell of shuttered rooms, old coffee and stagnant toilets. Desks had been abandoned in mid-task. The place felt ghostly, sinister. He found Zamir in the biggest room, which must be Lazaridis' office, where the shooting had occurred. Zamir was working on a big double filing cabinet behind the desk.

'Locked,' he said. 'One minute and it's open.' He slid a

large screwdriver from his pocket.

George checked the desk. He found an address book, a diary, a notepad with several pages of jottings. He opened the suitcase and dropped them in.

A metallic clang made him turn round.

'OK,' said Zamir. 'All yours. Now I'll find the safe.'

George worked quickly through the files. The tabs read like a *Who's Who* of Greek public life: politicians, singers, actors, shipowners, bankers... Any one of these could contain the clues to the lawyer's murder. He couldn't take them all. He flicked through, undecided, wondering where to begin. It was true about the adrenalin. He could feel his heart pumping. Then he spotted the name Kakridis.He lifted out the file and dropped it in his case.

He turned and looked around the office. No computer. That was odd. Surely a lawyer's office must have one. He hurried through to the other rooms. No computers there either. He checked behind the desks: there were all the connections, the multiplugs, the networking cables, the USBs. The place had been cleared of every piece of electronic equipment.

Zamir was working on a massive old iron safe in the next room. George was astonished to see that he was using nothing more complicated than a stethoscope.

'How long will that take?' he asked.

'I don't know. Can be minutes, can be hours. Maybe I will be lucky.'

'Do you know how to do that?'

'Of course. Please let me work. You keep looking around.'

'We're wasting our time. The computers have all gone.'

'I saw that. But please continue. We must use our time

to the maximum.' Zamir glanced at his watch. 'Ten minutes more. Then out.'

Despite the short deadline, George felt he was at a loose end. He walked through each of the rooms, trying to get a feel of the office hierarchy, and who might have held important documents. He settled on the secretary's office next to the director's. He opened the drawers in the desk, checked the waste-paper basket, found nothing there.

Suddenly the door opened. Haris was saying, 'Get out, quick! Up the stairs, onto the roof.'

'What's up?'

'Security staff.'

'How did…'

'Don't talk. Just go.'

George hurried out with his suitcase, climbed two short flights of stairs, and waited. The roof was still two floors up, but he wanted to see that Haris and Zamir were all right. From down below he heard shouts, running feet. A door slammed, then silence.

Where were Haris and Zamir?

Cautiously, he crept down the stairs again and approached the office door. He could hear voices inside, but whose were they? It was impossible to tell. He waited, uncertain what to do. Had things gone wrong, in spite of all Haris' planning?

Without warning the door flew open. Haris appeared, stopped in surprise, and said, 'Oh God you gave me a fright. You should be up on the roof!'

'You didn't follow. What's happened?'

Haris pulled George in and closed the door.

'There are two security guards in there. Tied to chairs. We

must get out now.'

'Where's Zamir?'

'Still trying to crack the safe.'

'He must stop.'

'I know. It's professional pride…'

'Come on. Let's go and get him.'

George led the way into the room where Zamir was bent in white-hot concentration, listening to the mechanism of the lock as he turned it, notch by notch, on the door of the safe. As they entered he gestured impatiently for them to be quiet.

George said, 'Come on, Zamir, time's up.'

'You go,' he said. 'I'll catch up.'

'No. You're coming with us. Now!'

'One more minute.'

George glanced at Haris, who nodded.

'All right. One minute.'

George checked his watch – 10:55:12 – the second hand hurrying blindly into the future, wiping out the past. *There's no chance he'll do it,* he thought.

He looked up and saw Haris staring at the top of a bookshelf by the window. Wondering what he had seen, he watched as Haris took a chair from a nearby desk, placed it under the bookshelf and climbed up. He ran his hand along the top and came down with a fat blue notebook in his hand. Opening it, he said, 'OK, let's have this.'

'What is it?'

'A diary.'

He flicked through to the date of the murder: February 10. There were the names of the visitors, their phone numbers, the business they came on. It was a secretary's diary, hastily hidden away before the office was cleared. There were many reasons to hide things, but this can only have been to keep compromising information out of the wrong hands.

What information? The names of the killers.

George opened his suitcase and shoved the diary in. As he did so Zamir let out a satisfied sigh and the door of the safe swung open. Inside were bundles of documents tied up with ribbon, envelopes, packages.

'Give me your case,' said Zamir.

'We can't take those,' said George.

'Maybe you can't. But I can.'

He reached for the case and quickly threw in the contents of the safe.

'OK,' he said. 'Now let's go.'

Zamir moved towards the door, carrying the heavily-laden suitcase lightly under one muscular arm. To George's surprise he headed up the stairs, not down.

George turned to Haris.

'Up?' he queried.

'That's our way out...'

Haris pulled the office door shut and they followed Zamir up the stairs.

At the end of the last flight a metal door led onto the roof and a spectacular view to the Acropolis and the sea. The whole city sparkled in the winter sunshine, and George felt, as every Athenian does from time to time, a surge of pride in the magnificence of the site, the dazzling sharpness and clarity of the light.

'Over there,' said Haris.

They crossed the roof to its far edge, where the safety rail stood close to that of a building in the next street. Zamir put down the suitcase and said, 'You first Mr Zafiris, then Mr Pezas. I throw the suitcase.'

George climbed up onto the railing, glimpsed the long drop between the buildings, and recoiled, his stomach fluttering. The gap looked too big to jump. He stepped down again and turned to Zamir.

'Have you done this?'

'Five times,' said Zamir.

'You're an acrobat.'

'It's about commitment, not profession.'

George looked down again, at the long cold shaft of air in which the force of gravity seemed to have multiplied exponentially, as if funnelled by the narrow space, to a horrible magnetic pull that drew his innards out of him.

'I can't do this,' he said. 'No chance. I'm going to use the stairs.'

'You can't go down the stairs,' said Haris. 'You'll be seen.'

'I'll show you,' said Zamir, clambering over the railing to the narrow concrete ledge. He crouched slightly and then flung himself out with an athletic lunge, hanging for a moment at full stretch above the abyss. His foot touched the parapet on the far side and he grabbed the rail.

He turned and said, 'You now, Mr Zafiris.'

He stretched out his hand. 'I'll catch you if you need me to.'

'What the hell,' said George and climbed the railing.

'Stand aside,' he told Zamir. 'I'll do it myself. Your hand doesn't help.'

Zamir withdrew his hand. George crouched, muttered

'God help me!' and jumped. He felt the void underneath him as he went, and part of him, a psychic presence, seemed to stay behind. But the air was rushing against his face and his body was in motion, crossing the space, and the far side came quickly towards him. His right shin hit the parapet, breaking his flight, he stumbled but grabbed with his left hand and caught the railing, twisted his body upwards wildly and his right hand gripped a metal post. He levered himself up with his knees and climbed over.

'Bravo,' said Zamir. Then, to Haris, 'Can you throw the suitcase?'

Haris picked it up and grunted. 'It's heavy.'

'Wait.'

Zamir jumped back across and told Haris to go.

George watched his assistant leap towards him as calmly as as a child jumping over a puddle.

'OK,' said Haris. 'Get ready to catch this thing.'

Zamir swung the case so that it came sailing towards them over the gap. Haris and George positioned themselves for the catch, fumbling its awkward weight but breaking its fall as it hit the flat concrete roof. Zamir nodded and hurried back to the door they had come through from the stairs.

'What's he doing?'

'Locking the door. Makes life a bit more difficult for the pursuer.'

Zamir was back in a few seconds. He jumped over the gap to join them.

'Now what?' said George.

'Down through this building and into the next street.'

'Is this door open?'

'Yes.'

'How come?'

Haris gestured to Zamir. 'The man who understands locks.'

Zamir picked up the suitcase. 'Let's go.'

35

Down in Omirou Street, George and Haris hailed a taxi and loaded the suitcase into the boot.

Zamir turned his leather jacket inside out – dark green to burgundy red – and walked off towards Panepistimiou.

'Where's he off to now?' asked George.

'Checking on his trucks. He'll join us at your place.'

'He's extremely thorough.'

'Of course.'

'So are you for that matter.'

Haris shrugged.

'That was a smooth piece of work. You just don't expect such things in our shambolic country.'

'*You* don't, George. I do, because I plan it all out, move by move.'

'The only thing I could have done without…'

'I know. It couldn't be helped. Zamir was sure you'd manage it. And he was right.'

'It's shortened my life by ten years.'

'You could have spent those years in prison.'

'That's still a possibility. God knows what's in the suitcase.'

'We'll see.'

The taxi dropped them outside 35 Aristotle Street – another Haris precaution – and they waited until it drove off before walking up to number 43. Inside the flat George made coffee while Haris began listing the contents of the suitcase.

'There are twelve envelopes here,' said Haris, 'all sealed.'

'Open them,' said George.

Haris took a pen knife from his pocket and slit the first envelope.

'OK,' he said. 'That's why Zamir was so keen. I'll bet he can smell this stuff.'

'What's that?'

'50,000 euros in this one, five packets of ten.'

'Open the others.'

George poured the coffee while Haris worked away with his knife.

'Another 50 here. And here… Looks like 600,000 in total. Jeez!'

'Don't let Zamir see it.'

'What are we going to do with it?'

'Hand it over to Sotiriou.'

'The whole lot?'

'We have to.'

'Do we?'

'I know what you're thinking.'

'Sotiriou has no idea what was in the safe, Lazaridis is dead…'

'The money isn't ours.'

'It soon could be!'

'Haris, you're thinking like an adolescent. Stop it! I'll take it into the bedroom before Zamir gets here.'

'He'll notice it's gone.'

'Let him.'

'Then he'll accuse you of theft. He can smell it, I tell you!'

'Tell you what, I'm going to call Sotiriou right now.'

'No, George, think first! You're up shit creek for money, so am I. Why not take it? No one's going to know a damn thing.'

'I've thought about it. Not just this time but many times before. It's about trust. If you let it go once, you're finished.'

'While everybody else is on the take! I don't think so.'

'I'm calling Sotiriou.'

'Please, no!'

George rang the number.

An impatient voice replied. 'Yes, what is it?'

'Colonel, we've visited…' George remembered that Sotiriou was convinced his phone was bugged '…the office you wanted us to visit.'

'Which one?'

'I went with Mr Zamir and Mr Pezas.'

'Ah yes. Satisfactory?'

'We're still alive.'

'Good.'

'We were able to retrieve several key documents. There was also a very large sum of money.'

'How large?'

'600,000 euros.'

'I see. What are you doing with it?'

'Asking your advice.'

'Can you bring it over?'

'Not now. A little later.'

'Good. Do that. I'll be here with the decorators.'

The call ended.

'I don't believe it,' said Haris. 'Such an opportunity!'

'Forget it, buddy. It's theft! I'm going to hide this cash now before the bloodhound gets here and makes me go through the whole damn business all over again.'

George sealed the envelopes with parcel tape and carried them into the bedroom, where he pushed them onto a shelf behind a pile of summer clothes. He returned to the kitchen, where Haris was still moping.

'Just imagine for a moment that it was your safe,' said George. 'How would you feel about someone else helping himself to your money?'

'Lazaridis is dead!'

'What about his family? His employees? The money could be theirs.'

'I know. You're right in principle. It's just… What's the point of principles when the whole of society is dedicated to selfishness and opportunism?'

'That's when we most need principles, Haris! In unstable times, when every idiot is trumpeting the beauty of change, we must hold fast to the good.'

'And suffer for it!'

'Remember, my friend: *we may have smashed their statues and driven them out of their temples, but the old gods never died.*'

'They died long ago. All that's left is winners and losers.'

'OK, see it that way if you want. So you've lost! Accept it. "Suck it up, princess", as they say in America.'

'I wouldn't mind if I was a princess. Or in America.'

'Let's get on with the job, shall we?'

They spent the next two hours going through the papers. At the end of that time, they had isolated four items of special interest: the diary entries for the day of the Lazaridis murder; the articles of association of a holding company based in Cyprus from the file of Simeon Yerakas; a letter from the Minister of Development, Byron Kakridis, stating that he wished to sue an investigative journalist, together with a curt reply from Lazaridis declining to take on such an obviously weak case; and a note on the jotter pad on the subject of *Non-EU migrant workers' rights*. There was no mention anywhere of 600,000 euros in cash.

At two o'clock, Zamir arrived. He was in high spirits, and very hungry. 'All my boys safely home, the trucks in the garage, but no food in the belly. I need to eat.'

'We can go to the café downstairs.'

He cast his eyes over the documents on the kitchen table.

'Anything useful?' he asked.

'A few things,' said George.

'The envelopes?'

'You tell him, Haris,' said George wearily.

Haris explained, while Zamir listened in growing astonishment. 'If God opens a door, it's your duty to go through it,' he said. 'When there's *cash* on the other side, you go even faster…'

'I stick with the commandment *Thou shalt not steal.*'

'Why did you come with us this morning, Mr Zafiris? We were stealing!'

'Under police orders. In the public interest. I'd call it "liberation", not "theft".'

'I always call it liberation.'

'You're a special case.'

'We're all special cases! All short of cash. Let's go before I eat this table.'

Down at the Café Agamemnon they ordered three beers and a big platter of *souvlakia* and chips from the local taverna. While sipping their beer, Haris asked after Zoe.

'She's away,' said George.

'Where?'

'Andros.'

'Why?'

'I wish I knew. Normally she goes there to paint and relax. This time it's to get away from me.'

'How long will she stay?'

'I don't know. A few months?'

'Have you quarrelled?'

'Only every day for the past ten years.'

'About what?'

'Money. Success. Status. Our son. The family. Any subject you can think of, we disagree about it.'

'Sounds familiar.'

'Same for you?'

'Mine is threatening to walk out.'

'Why?'

'Money. Success. Status. Our son…'

'Oh dear. Try to stop her going.'

'I would, but I made things worse recently by taking in that Scottish girl and her two kids.'

'Haris, you're crazy. Why did you do that?'

'I couldn't stand to see her so miserable.'

'And your wife's furious?'

'Totally. "Who is this *puttana?*" All the usual stuff.'

'Are you sleeping with her?'

'That one too.'

'No, but are you?'

Haris was indignant. 'No! I'm just doing a good turn.'

'Your wife sees it differently.'

'Of course. She just sees a threat, an inconvenience… I just wish I could find someone else to take her in. She's no trouble, so grateful, and the kids are sweet.'

'How about you, Zamir?'

Zamir was absorbed in his phone. 'What's that?'

'Could you take in a Scottish girl and her two children?'

Zamir's eyes lit up. 'If she's good looking, and not too proud…'

'What would your wife say?'

'Nothing. She would just take the biggest kitchen knife and stick it first in the girl, then in me.'

'What about you, George? You have an empty flat now.'

'I know. It's just…'

'What? Your wife?'

'Just like yours.'

'But she's off! How will it bother her?'

'She'll find a way.'

'I wish you'd do it. You'd help the girl and you'd help me.'

'Let me think about it,' said George. 'I'm pretty sure my wife would move back in just to stop it.'

After lunch, Zamir and Haris went off their separate ways, while George returned to the flat to collect the suitcase and the envelopes of cash. While he was in the bedroom, ignoring the siren voices that told him to keep a few thousand for himself, his telephone rang.

'Mr Zafiris, this is Sonia Venieri.'

'Good afternoon, Miss Venieri. What's new?'

'I want to apologise for my behaviour yesterday.'

'There's no need.'

'I was ungrateful.'

'It's no problem.'

'I hope you don't think badly of me for it.'

'Not at all.'

'I also thought I should tell you I'm changing job.'

'Really?'

'I'm being transferred to Crete.'

'Crete? Why?'

'To get me out of Athens, obviously!'

'When?'

'Immediately.'

'And your investigations?'

'I'm to leave everything as it is. Someone else will take over my cases.'

'That's sudden,' said George.

'You bet.'

'I'm sorry.'

'Of course we know who's behind it,' she said.

'Do we?'

'I'm not going to say the name. It's someone we've talked about.'

'I understand,' said George.

He thought for a moment or two. 'Is there no appeal?'

'Appeal? I'm being *purged*. I can count myself lucky not to get worse treatment.'

'I'll do what I can to help,' said George. 'And you must keep up the struggle.'

'I will.'

'Let me know how it goes in Crete.'

'Thank you. It's exile, but I'll make it count.'

George returned to the cash-filled envelopes, thinking *That's the reward for honesty.*

36

As soon as he saw the suitcase in George's hand, Colonel Sotiriou sent the decorators out for a coffee. Accustomed to his whims and abrupt commands, the two men happily laid down their brushes and stepped outside.

The Colonel cleared a space on his desk. 'Come on,' he said, 'Let's see what you've got.'

George swung the case up onto the desk, snapped the catches and flipped back the lid.

'You've been through it all?' enquired the Colonel.

George nodded. He handed over the diary and the other documents he had singled out. 'These are what interest me in particular.'

'No laptops, hard drives, memory sticks?'

'All missing.'

'Of course. They're not total amateurs after all... Tell me, what's so special about the holding company?'

'It may be nothing. I just think it might lead somewhere.'

'And the letter from Kakridis?'

'Ditto. It's all about tax avoidance. With your permission I would like to copy these and take the investigation one stage further.'

'You don't need my permission.'

'Call it "commission" then.'

'Ah. You want paying?'

'I do. Unlike you, Colonel, I don't receive a salary.'

'I must think about that. So many projects to co-ordinate, such a multiplicity of calls on my time, attention, resources…' The Colonel drifted off for a moment into other thoughts, his eyes becoming distant and vague. Then suddenly he was back. He picked up one of the envelopes. 'I see you've brought the cash. Is this the original amount?'

'Untouched.'

'The envelopes have been opened.'

'Only to check the contents.'

'Zamir didn't help himself?'

'I wouldn't let him.'

The Colonel's eyebrows rose briefly. 'How about you? Did you not think of taking something for yourself? It would have been extremely easy.'

'Please, Colonel! I've explained it to Pezas and Zamir. It was like talking to children. Surely I don't have to explain it to you!'

'Don't get shirty, Zafiris! Some people – most people in fact – would just take it and say nothing.'

'No doubt. But this money clearly belongs to someone.'

'Who?'

'I haven't the faintest idea, but it was in a *safe*! *A lawyer's safe!* That suggests a certain interest in hanging onto it.'

'I don't dispute that. But without a name, how can this cash be returned to its owner? And what if the owner is a criminal? This could be bribe money! *Rousfeti!*'

'Colonel, with respect, you're talking like a delinquent. What you're doing in the police force God only knows!'

The Colonel placed his hand on George's arm. 'Relax,' he said. 'I do actually have some understanding of the moral issues.'

'Congratulations. You must be the only official in this country who does!'

'I need to absorb this material,' said the Colonel, his mind hurrying on. 'It must never be traced to this office.' He opened his own safe hidden in the bookshelves and lodged the envelopes carefully inside.

'I'll have copies made of the documents you want, and get straight on to that list of names from the diary.' He closed the safe, turned and straightened up. 'That is really excellent work. Zamir and Pezas performed well?'

'Outstanding. Planning and execution impeccable. Somehow that mixture of special forces and circus is… how can I put it? Surreal but effective.'

Sotiriou nodded. 'I suspected as much. Now tell me, what do I owe you for all this?'

'We said seventy-five for the lot. Fifty for Zamir and his trucks, twenty-five for me and Haris. You've given me ten already.'

The Colonel returned to the safe, took out two of the envelopes, slashed the parcel tape with a desk knife and counted out 65,000 euros. He added another 5,000 and handed the pile of notes to George

'What's the extra five for?'

'The next phase of research.'

'Aren't those the banknotes I've just given you?'

'They may be. Why?'

'They could be traced by the serial numbers'

The Colonel put out his hand. 'You're right,' he said. 'Let me give you some others.'

He pulled a fresh bundle of banknotes from his safe and counted them out.

'Off you go now,' he said. 'Find out what you can. I'll get to work on the diary.'

On the way home, as the setting sun turned the sea between Corinth and Athens into a vast cauldron of gold, tinting the western slopes of Hymettus and dissolving the ships and mountains into purple shadows, George was overwhelmed with sorrow and wonder. Sorrow at his troubles with Zoe, the prospect of a solitary life. Wonder at the light, the majestic landscape. As the sun dipped towards the horizon, the Peloponnese and Ionian land beyond, bringing an end to this day and twilight to his marriage, he grieved in his soul for the time that was lost. They had fought their way to a point of no return. Both stood up for what they believed was right. Their disagreements were born of deep convictions. How could they ever agree? And without agreement, how could they ever live in the same house again? He remembered the happy years, a time when their minds were in harmony. So much laughter. So much love. Those things remained, preserved in memory, his son and wife in earlier days. *They love you still,* he told himself, *their spirits remember you still.* Had she changed so much since then? Had he? Was there no compromise to be found? No way back?

His phone started ringing.

'Hello, George.'

'Zoe. I was thinking about you.'

'Where are you?'

'Walking home through Kolonaki.'

'George, I've decided not to come back. Not for a month or two anyway. I want to try living apart.'

'I understand.'

'I think it's best for me. I don't know about you.'

'I'd prefer not, but it takes two.'

'Surely you don't think we can go on?'

'Probably not.'

'Something has to change.'

'I agree.'

'If our minds won't change, our lives must.'

'Correct.'

'I can leave Athens, you can't, so you use the flat, I'll use the house in Andros.'

'Shall I bring your things?'

'No. I'll arrange that.'

'OK… I can't tell you how sad this makes me.'

'Not sad enough to change, though?'

He thought about this. Although gently spoken, it was, he felt, a piece of emotional blackmail. Throwing the guilt onto him. He tried to stay calm.

'No,' he said. 'Not sad enough to change.'

37

A week passed. A week of loneliness, feelings of failure and bitter remorse. Lines from Dante, read long ago, resurfaced in his mind with a lacerating fire:

Nessun maggior dolore
che ricordarsi del tempo felice
ne la miseria.

It was as if nothing had developed in his life, nothing grown to fruition, except loss. When Nick phoned and asked how he was, George told him what had happened. He tried to contain the sorrow, avoiding all blame.

Nick said sorrowfully, 'I feel I was the cause of this.'

'Never think that,' said George. 'Your mother and I have been moving apart for years. It's nothing to do with you. Your career was just another thing we disagreed about. And I hold firm in my belief that it's *your* choice, not ours.'

'Give it a few months, dad. When I get my first pay packet, things will look better.'

'Wise words, Nick. You may well be right.'

'Keep your pecker up.'

'Thanks. You too. We'll speak soon...'

To keep depression at bay, he went running every day around the wooded slopes of Lycabettus, relishing the cool February sunshine that blazed through the leafless trees, the glimpses of the Acropolis and the glittering seascape beyond. Back at the flat he threw himself into his work, investigating Yerakas and his Cypriot holding company, digging out the article that had caused such offence to Kakridis, and looking into the tax affairs of both men. In this Sonia Venieri was able to help, despite her move to Crete. She informed him that neither of them, two of the richest men in Greece, paid more than €10,000 in tax each year. George was surprised they paid any tax at all.

Gradually he put together a picture. The holding company controlled a group of smaller companies, which in turn held shares in single enterprise concerns, all related to property in some form. As well as the enterprises George already knew about – the hotels and tourist resorts – there were also public relations agencies, joint ventures with Israeli and Russian developers, farms, factories, and a business dedicated to raising grants from the government and the European Union. Did any of this have to do with the death of Lazaridis? Or of Wasim Khan? He could trace no causal line between them, but his instinct told him it was there.

One morning, as he revolved the case in his mind, it occurred to him to call Yiannis Koroneos, his lawyer, and ask what he knew about Lazaridis. A fellow professional might well have some inside knowledge. Even gossip could be useful.

Yiannis said he knew Lazaridis well. Liked him, even sympathised with his famous 'change of heart'. George asked him what he meant by this. Yiannis told him that for twenty years Lazaridis had been 'the attorney to the stars', with all the

266

attendant benefits: a yacht, a house on Mykonos and a flat in Paris. Then the country's crisis had got to him. He caught 'the bug of socialism', only it wasn't political socialism, it was a generalised sympathy for the underdog, a belief that everything in life, good and bad, should be shared more equally across society. He complained that the country's ills were being paid for by the innocent, the 'small people', while the guilty continued to live in their old selfish and corrupt ways.

'I'm sure you get the picture,' said Yiannis.

'It sounds like a perfectly sensible reaction.'

'Of course. Many of us share his views, but we're all struggling so hard to stay afloat that we have no time to think of anyone else.'

'How did he manage it?'

'He was rich. And brave.'

'Active?'

'Very. And he paid the price.'

'Did he have any interest in immigrant workers?'

'He did. And refugees. He helped them for free. Caused great upset among his colleagues.'

'What harm is there in that?'

'It undercuts fees! Cheapens the profession!'

'Even when it's done for charity?'

'You'd be surprised how petty-minded people can be.'

'Did he upset anyone enough to have him killed?'

'Hard to say. Possibly.'

'How did his star clients like the new style?'

'Some supported him. The artists, a few top academics and business people, the ones with vision.'

'And the rest?'

'Indifferent.'

'Anyone really angry?'

'Sorry, George, I just don't know. It would be logical for some of those clients to feel threatened, but whether in a personal way, and who they might be, I can't say.'

He was pondering this when a call came through from Sotiriou, asking him to come into the office. The Colonel would not say what it was about – he never did – but they agreed a time in the early afternoon.

As soon as that call ended, another one came in.

'Don't tell me a joke please, Haris, I can't laugh any more.'

'Neither can I. My laughing days are over.'

'What's up?'

'Things are bad, George.'

'Tell me.'

'My wife has given me an ultimatum.'

'I have just one word of advice. Capitulate!'

'I have to ask Margaret and her kids to leave.'

'Who is Margaret?'

'The Scottish girl.'

'That's the way it goes, buddy. Zamir told you. I told you. You can't have two women in the same house.'

'Have you had a chance to consider it?'

'What?'

'Putting them up.'

'Did I say I would?'

'You said you'd think about it.'

'I'm sorry, Haris. It's been such turmoil here…'

'Can you think about it now? Urgently?'

Again George wanted to say *Let me think about it,* but the time for that was past.

'What's stopping you?'

'I don't know. Just… Damn it, does she have no other options?'

'She can go back to the hell of her marriage, her evil mother-in-law, her lout of a husband… Or say good bye to her children. Those are the alternatives.'

'It's coming back to me.'

'Why not give it a try? Just for a week?'

'You put me in a difficult position, Haris!'

'Really? You're miserable living alone, you've said so yourself, you've got a nice flat which is too big, you'll be doing her an enormous favour…'

'It just seems weird! And sudden.'

'Forget weird and sudden, George! These are crazy times. Weird things happen every day. We need to help each other! Hell, man, I'd do it! In fact I *have* done it, and it's nearly cost me my marriage. But I don't regret it, because it's the right thing to do, and my wife's just acting up out of totally unfounded jealousy and selfishness.'

'It's what every woman would do, Haris!'

'I don't give a shit. I want to help! And you've got a chance now to make a difference to someone's life. You've got no nagging wife to worry about. You're free. If you don't do it I'll be bloody disappointed and think you're a selfish prick like every other complacent piece of shit I know.'

'I've never even met this woman!'

'She's a fine person, I promise you. No trouble. Give it a try, boss, please! Just for one lousy week!'

'I don't believe this,' said George.

'I hope that means yes.'

'I'm going crazy here.'

'You won't regret it. In fact you'll thank me. Let me bring her over to meet you.'

'Oh bugger it. Against my better judgement, and just to shut you up, I'll meet her. But I promise nothing. Absolutely nothing!'

'You're a prince, boss. A man in a million!'

With Haris' importunate words echoing in his ears, he gathered up his research notes and set out to see Sotiriou. After a brisk 20-minute walk through the city, he found the Colonel in his newly decorated office, the stacks of files still on the floor but now piled up neatly, several deep, against one wall.

'This looks better,' said George.

The Colonel grimaced. 'I had a system once. It was idiosyncratic but functional. Now I can't find anything. And so the forces of chaos and disruption continue their triumphant course through our national institutions!'

'They find a formidable obstacle in you, Colonel.'

'Not formidable enough I fear.'

'You asked to see me.'

'I want a progress report.'

George took him through his research. Showed him a diagram of the holding companies, the network of single enterprises, the tax figures. Sotiriou absorbed it all in grim silence.

'None of this is criminal in itself,' he said finally.

'I realise that,' said George, 'but it's typically cloudy stuff, designed to confuse and baulk any form of inquiry or –'

The Colonel held up his hand. 'Stop, Zafiris! What possible relevance does this have to me? Remember I deal with violent crime, not just "cloudy stuff"!'

'I'm coming to that.'

'Get on with it!'

'We have two murders and one attempted rape. Violent enough for you, I trust?'

Sotiriou waved this away.

George went on: 'Each of the victims represented a threat to the three people at the heart of this.'

'Kakridis, Yerakas and… who is the third?'

'Katramis.'

'You think they're connected?'

'I know they are! I've seen them together.'

'But how do we know they had anything to do with these specific crimes?'

'Wasim was killed on a farm owned by Yerakas. Sonia Venieri was attacked by two men using Maria Katramis' car…'

'She claims it was stolen.'

'Naturally.'

'It could be true.'

'Is there any evidence it was stolen?'

'No, but that doesn't disprove her claim.'

'How did the thieves get into the car? How did they start it?'

Sotiriou shrugged his shoulders. 'They were professionals.'

'Can a professional get into a car, and start it, without leaving any traces?'

'Of course. There are relay devices, hacking programmes,

stolen keys…'

'OK, that may be tricky to pin on her, but let me go on. Lazaridis was becoming notorious for his radical views.'

'You think someone killed him for his *views*? That's a hell of a stretch.'

'Look at how he treated Kakridis when he wanted to sue an investigative journalist. "Don't attempt this," he wrote. "It would be wiser to act more ethically and put your affairs in order than to threaten journalists." Lazaridis knew these people's secrets, but he was no longer willing to protect them. That amounts to a threat, doesn't it? Or a betrayal. Which is worse.'

'As a lawyer he had an obligation of confidentiality.'

'In the face of crimes? Doesn't the law require us to divulge felonies? Even if we are made aware of them in confidence?'

'No!' said Sotiriou. 'Confidentiality rules! If a lawyer is asked to represent someone and then discovers that this person is guilty, he must decline the case – not report it to the police. That is the law. Regrettably, in my view, but that's the way it is.'

'You don't believe Lazaridis was a threat?'

'I'm not saying that! His knowledge was certainly dangerous.'

'So how do we proceed?'

Sotiriou thought about this for a few moments.

'I'm in two minds,' he said. 'My approach to these cases is always cautious. The big players have big lawyers to defend them. Any flaw in the evidence, any doubt in the witnesses, the tiniest inconsistency in your reasoning, and you're finished. They'll escape through the smallest crack, like the cockroaches they resemble in so many ways. What we have gathered so far is a long way from a proper case. To do this properly we need documentation, witness statements, recordings of telephone calls, and so on. That will take a team of investigators many months of work. It's too much for you… If I go ahead my first act will necessarily be to take this case off your hands.'

George felt the stirrings of anger. 'So that's it? Case closed for five years while the officials sit on it, constipating the whole thing, then the statute of limitations comes in and suddenly there's no case for these bastards to answer. Is that how you solve the country's problems?'

'Hold on, Zafiris. I share your frustration, but I have to work with the system. I'll tell you this, though. If you're willing to accompany me, I should like to visit Mr Yerakas at his farm at Marathon, meet the man face to face, confront him about the one thing we do know for certain, that Wasim Khan died by violence on his land. What do you say?'

'If you think it will help.'

'I wouldn't suggest it otherwise.'

'Will he meet us?'

'I'm sure he will.'

George was puzzled. 'Why do you want to do this?'

The Colonel shifted in his chair. 'Good question. I've been sitting at this desk for the past twelve years, watching cases come and go, watching *you* come and go, feeling ever more distant from our real work. I'm an administrator now. I sit among papers, emails, phone calls. Getting older, feeling 'weary, stale, flat and unprofitable' as Shakespeare puts it, as if nothing is really happening any longer. You know that feeling, when you're young, it's high summer and you sleep under the stars, it's a night of animal noises, strange lights and dreams, and you're aware of great cosmic energies around you, and then as an August morning dawns over you, you feel their life-force enter your being?'

'It's a long time since I felt that!'

'Same for me. But you know what I mean? I'm tired of this half-life. This entropy, this stifling atmosphere of systems, procedures, codes, records, files! I have the most imperious urge to return to the world of action, to feel the pulse of pursuit, the electricity, the live charge of risk as you question a suspect and balance the light in his eyes with the light in yours… Do I make myself clear?'

'Perfectly.'

'Good! I'll make the arrangements. One evening this week, I suggest.'

George stood up, mild doubts about the Colonel's sanity flickering through his mind. A knock on the door made him turn.

'Yes!'

A young officer hurried in.

'What is it?' asked the Colonel.

'There's been a shooting down in Glyfada.'

'Anything special?'

'There's an American involved.'

'Victim or perpetrator?'

'Possibly both.'

'Explain yourself!'

'He was jumped outside his office by two men. They tried to kill him, but he was armed and managed to defend himself.'

'Where is he now?'

'In hospital.'

'Will he live?'

'Yes.'

'How about his attackers?'

'They got away, but he says he hit one of them.'

'All right,' said the Colonel. 'Thanks for the report. Keep me posted.'

'There's something else I have to tell you, sir.'

'Go on then!'

'He says your visitor was involved.'

'Which visitor?'

The officer indicated George.

'In what way?'

'He claims Mr Zafiris threatened him.'

'Really? When?'

'Eight days ago.' The officer took a notebook from his pocket. *I was telephoned by a private detective, Mr Zafiris, on behalf of his client Katramis Construction. He requested that I cease trading in competition with his client or face punishment.'*

The Colonel turned to George. 'Is that true, Mr Zafiris?'

George felt a sudden chill in the room. He knew he must be careful in his reply.

'I spoke to an American businessman several days ago,' he said, 'on behalf of Katramis Construction. That much is true. But I didn't ask him to cease trading, or threaten him with punishment.'

'So why did you call him?'

'To seek co-operation.'

'Why didn't Katramis do that himself?'

'I don't know. Maybe they've tried already. He wasn't an easy man to deal with.'

Sotiriou turned to the officer.

'Is there a recording of the call?'

'There is.'

'Have you heard it?'

'No, sir.'

'Get hold of it at once.'

'Yes, sir.'

'Meanwhile I will vouch for Mr Zafiris.'

'I should strictly arrest him.'

'I know that! I am relieving you of that duty.'

'Will you arrest him, sir?'

'Let me hear the recording first.'

'Very good, sir.'

The officer left the room.

'You'd better go now,' said the Colonel, 'in case I find out you're lying.'

38

Back in Aristotle Street, George tidied the flat in preparation for the Scottish woman's visit. He was still not keen on the idea of housing a troubled mother and her two small children, but Haris' plea had moved him. He had thought about it and decided there was no harm in it; potentially some good. He owed a huge, unpayable debt to Haris over the death of his brother Hector. Haris never referred to this, never came near to using it, but George felt Hector's presence, and the pain of his loss, every single day.

Zoe would be angry, but she was angry about everything anyway; so, as the English proverb put it, *he might as well be hanged for a sheep as for a lamb.*

Just before six, with everything in place, his phone rang.

'*Yiorgo?* It's me.'

'Hello, Maria,' he said coldly.

'I got your message.'

'Obviously.'

'And I wanted…' She stopped. 'Why do you say "obviously"?'

'Is that how you treat everyone who crosses you? Either exile or violence?'

'What are you talking about, George?'

'The Greek-American, Jerry Kasimatis.'

'What about him?'

'Come on, Maria, you know just as well as I do.'

'I don't know anything about him.'

'Of course. You send a pair of hit-men to take him out, but you don't know anything about him? He's just a stranger?'

'George, I swear…'

'The police have me down as a suspect.'

'If I knew…'

'For heaven's sake, Maria! Can't you stop lying for a moment? To yourself and the world? And at some point just *think about what you're doing?* If you weren't Zoe's cousin I would shop you straightaway.'

'George, you've lost your mind!'

'Who sent those men? You or Yerakas?'

'I wish you'd explain!'

George still didn't believe her, but he explained anyway. Maria listened attentively.

'Well,' she said at last. 'It seems that something sank in.'

'What do you mean?'

'Kasimatis called Stelios this afternoon.'

'And?'

'He wants to do business.'

'You're kidding!'

'No. He said he wants to talk. "Because co-operation is better than aggression".'

'My very words to him.'

'You see? Your efforts weren't wasted.'

George felt disgusted. His efforts seemed little more than

a sideshow.

'So what happens now, Maria? We're all friends?'

'We'll see. Stelios is very pleased. Things had to change. Those Americans undercutting us, hovering like vultures, waiting for us to die... They're evil people! Arrogant people! They think the whole world exists for their convenience.'

How true of you as well, he thought.

At that moment the doorbell rang.

'I have to go, Maria. I'm expecting someone.'

'Go! I just wanted to tell you the news.'

George hung up and hurried to the front door. He buzzed the visitors in. Standing in his open doorway he heard the voices of children as they climbed the stairs. How long it was since that sound last echoed in the building!

Haris led the group, reached the landing first, and nodded to George, muttering, 'Thanks, buddy. You can't believe how grateful I am to you for this.'

The young woman and her children followed: she in her thirties, an ethereal young form, wary, with nervous eyes, the children three or four years old at most, bubbling with questions. George showed them into the sitting room and offered them all a drink.

'Just water,' said the mother. 'Thank you.'

They discussed how this stay might work. George showed Margaret the spare room and wondered where the children would sleep. She said they could share her bed for now. He showed her the kitchen and bathroom. She said it was all 'very nice and clean' and asked him how much he wanted. Taken aback, he said, 'Nothing. Not for this week. If it works, we can settle on some modest rent, but I know you have problems, so let's not add the worry of money.'

She thanked him and asked about his domestic situation. He explained, telling her about Nick in England and Zoe in Andros, describing her absence as 'a temporary break'. She listened somewhat blankly, no doubt thinking of her own worse circumstances.

'Are you OK with that?' he asked.

'Oh yes,' she said. 'I just hoped it would be all right with your wife.'

'I haven't told her anything yet,' he said. 'But I will.'

Margaret asked if she could prepare meals for the children in the kitchen.

'Of course,' said George. 'Use the place as if it were your own.'

Within half an hour it was all arranged. A slight uneasiness remained, something indistinct, but George put this down to the inherent strangeness of the situation, as well as the woman's all too visible psychological wounds. How could she know that she and her children were safe? That he wasn't a predator? It was a gamble. She had Haris' word, nothing more. George found himself not being too friendly, in case it was taken wrongly. You never knew with the Brits. Cautious people.

Haris went down to fetch the bags while George, remembering his life as a young father and the concerns about safety that accompanied those years, went round the apartment putting delicate and dangerous things out of children's reach. He ended his tour at the desk, which he carefully locked. He did not want the children playing with his cameras, or his laptop, or his gun.

The next day Colonel Sotirou called: Yerakas would see them at seven that evening. They would leave police headquarters at six. George should be there by quarter to.

'Any news of the recording?' asked George.

'Which one?'

'Me and the American.'

'Ah yes.'

'You've heard it?'

'I have. Several times. You came very close to threatening him.'

'I was trying to broker peace.'

'Really? Is that what Katramis asked you to do?'

'It's a complicated story. Katramis believes the Americans are undermining his business.'

'Are they?'

'Most certainly.'

'How?'

'Malicious rumours, reputation damage. And undercutting their prices.'

'So Katramis hired you to get them off his back?'

'More or less.'

'That phone call was your attempt to do that?'

'It was.'

Sotiriou seemed amused. 'You didn't get very far, did you?'

'No,' said George.

'I'm surprised you didn't threaten him a great deal more.'

'Where does this go from here?' asked George.

'I must decide whether to arrest you or not.'

'What's your inclination?'

'To throw you into preventive detention until we clear this all up.'

'What will that achieve?'

'It might prevent an international incident.'

'OK,' said George. 'What am I supposed to do?'

'Stick to your line about brokering peace.'

'It has the advantage of being true.'

'Don't be too sure.'

'I know what I said, and what I meant.'

'Luckily, Zafiris, you stopped short of an explicit threat, or just short enough to allow me some discretion. Which I am prepared to exercise for the sake of our other work.'

'Any luck with finding the attackers?'

'No. The description doesn't match anyone we know. But if Katramis sent those men I'm going after him. And no mercy will be shown. To him or you.'

George changed the subject.

'Can we forget about this for now? Seeing as we have work to do this evening?'

'Gladly.'

'What's our back-up for the Marathon visit?'

''There's no back-up,' said the Colonel.

'Why not?'

'It's an unofficial call. I don't expect trouble. Do you?'

'I've learned to expect it.'

'You'll be armed?'

'Just my Beretta. How about you?'

'My driver's armed. We'll be fine.'

George was not so sure. He remembered Haris' warnings about knowing your target and planning for the unforeseen.

He called Haris and asked if he could join them,

'Of course,' said Haris. 'What's going on?'

George explained.

'You were right to call me,' said Haris. 'I'll be there.'

That evening at quarter to six they met outside the police headquarters. Sotiriou came down to meet them, and led the way to a grey unmarked Citroën whose driver jumped out smartly to open the doors for them. They drove out to Nea Makri, discussing the plan of approach.

'I want to keep this personal and informal,' said Sotiriou. 'Totally non-threatening, that's the idea.'

'I'll stay in the background,' said Haris.

'Good.'

'Tell me the set-up.'

George described the Yerakas estate. Haris asked questions about doors and windows and security arrangements while the Colonel grew increasingly impatient.

'Mr Pezas!' he finally burst out. 'It is not my intention to carry out a military siege! I want to keep the whole thing very simple!'

'Change it!' said Haris. 'Simplicity is only achieved by careful planning.'

'It's your mentality that I find disturbing, Mr Pezas. If we go in expecting a fight we will undoubtedly get one.'

Haris bristled angrily. 'If you don't want my help I'll go home.'

'Fine by me!' said Sotiriou.

'Not by me!' said George.

'Which is it to be?'

'My men are a phone call away,' said Sotiriou. 'You may as well go home.'

'It'll take your men an hour to get out there,' snapped George. 'Haris, you must stay!'

'I can't do both.'

'Stay!'

'Go! You're surplus to requirements. You'll ruin everything.'

'Mr Zafiris is right,' said Haris. 'You want to be in a position of strength. We can decide afterwards if I was surplus to requirements.'

'I'm not happy,' said Sotiriou.

'Pardon me, sir,' said the driver. 'He can stay with me. Then you have us in reserve in case of necessity.'

'That's a good plan,' said Sotiriou.

They had reached the gate of the farm.

Simeon Yerakas was waiting outside the main door. He was dressed in a maroon velvet jogging suit and matching trainers, with a purple and yellow cravat at his throat. The silver undulations of his hair were perfectly groomed, his welcome formal and unsmiling. He invited them coldly in.

'Let the driver come in too,' he said. 'He can go to the staff kitchen.' Then, seeing Haris, 'Who is this?'

'He is Mr Zafiris' assistant,' said the Colonel.

'I wasn't expecting so many of you!'

'A last minute addition.'

Yerakas looked him up and down, then said quietly, 'Very well, come in.'

He led them into a large, wood-panelled office, furnished

with quiet luxury. He indicated a sofa, upholstered in olive-green leather, opposite the desk.

'Sit down, gentlemen. Make yourselves comfortable. Tell me, Colonel, what can I do for you?'

'A farm worker named Wasim Khan was killed on your estate in January,' said Sotiriou. 'Nothing was reported to the local police, it was as if the man never existed. When my colleague here, Mr Zafiris, attempted to make inquiries he was attacked by one of your supervisors with a cudgel blow to the head. That too might well have been fatal had he not been lucky.'

'I'm sorry to hear it,' said Yerakas.

'You may well be even sorrier.'

'I shall make the necessary enquiries.'

'It's too late for that. We need to speak to your son Sebastian, and to the supervisor in question.'

'That will be difficult.'

'Why?'

'We're very busy here.'

'We're all busy, Mr Yerakas!' said Sotiriou aggressively.

Yerakas went on, unperturbed: 'I find your tone rather odd, Colonel, and your methods irregular. You should be issuing the proper warnings and following correct procedures.'

'There weren't too many of those when Wasim Khan was killed,' said George. 'Or when I was hit on the head.'

'I was not aware of any of this,' said Yerakas firmly. 'All I can do is look into it.'

'We've told you what you can do,' said Sotiriou. 'Now kindly do it.'

Yerakas reacted angrily. 'You are exceeding your powers,

Colonel! I have a good mind to make a formal complaint to the Minister of Justice – who is a personal friend.'

'Just get your son in here, and that supervisor, and we'll see about complaints afterwards,' said Sotiriou.

Yerakas stared at him coldly. Sotiriou glared hotly back. Yerakas picked up the phone and said softly, 'Mihali, please ask Sebastian to come to the office with Manolis and the team.'

'We don't need the team,' said Sotiriou.

'Let's do this properly,' said Yerakas

A minute later the door opened and Mihalis, the security chief, led in Sebastian, the farm supervisor Manolis and five of his 'team', all big, mean-looking, steroidal types. One, George noticed, had a bandaged hand.

Yerakas introduced the visitors. His son and Mihalis shook hands with them, the others barely acknowledging their presence. Yerakas invited Colonel Sotiriou to repeat the accusations, which he did with forceful simplicity.

'Manolis,' said Yerakas, 'since you are in charge of the farm day-to-day, please respond.'

The supervisor replied contemptuously, 'I've never heard of this "Kamikaze Khan".'

George corrected him on the name.

'What about your team?' asked Yerakas.

Manolis put it to them. The team were silent.

'Answer the question!' snapped Sotiriou.

'Do as the Colonel says,' said Yerakas.

One by one they said, 'No.'

Yerakas turned to the Colonel. 'So much for the first accusation. As to the second, did any of you hit this gentleman here with a cudgel?'

Again a series of denials.

'I'm afraid it looks as if we can't help you,' said Yerakas.

'They're lying,' said George. 'The supervisor was there when I was attacked. So was Sebastian. They saw it happen.'

'Sebastian?' said Yerakas solemnly. 'Is this true?'

'I was there,' said Sebastian, 'but I didn't see anyone hit Mr Zafiris.'

'Perhaps you hit him yourself,' said the Colonel.

'I don't carry any weapons.'

'You could have borrowed one!'

'I did not hit him.'

'You say you didn't see anyone hit Mr Zafiris? Let's go over this carefully. One moment he was standing talking to you, the next he was lying unconscious on the ground, and you didn't see anything? That's beyond belief. In fact it's ridiculous.'

'I was distracted.'

'By what?'

'There was an aeroplane, a small biplane flying quite low. I turned to look, watched it for a while, and when I turned back Mr Zafiris was on the ground.'

'You didn't hear anything? You didn't see anyone standing over him?'

'No.'

'Where was the supervisor?'

'I forget exactly where, but he was not near Mr Zafiris.'

'Was there anyone else there?'

'Possibly. I can't remember.'

'It was only two weeks ago!'

'If I could remember I would say so.'

The Colonel turned to George. 'What do you remember?'

'I was talking to Sebastian, and suddenly – bang.'

'You were hit from behind?'

'Yes.'

'When you were talking to Sebastian could you also see Manolis?'

'I can't remember.'

'Were any of these others present?'

'I think they were.'

'How many?'

'Two or three.'

'Can you identify which ones?'

George cast his eye along the line. 'I think those two at the end,' he said. 'Nearest the door.' They included the man with the bandaged hand.

'It follows that one of those two, or Manolis the supervisor, must have hit you?'

'Yes.'

Yerakas intervened. 'This is highly tendentious, Colonel! We have the uncertain testimony of a man who was struck on the head by something or someone, with an imprecise number of witnesses. He is confused in his memories.'

'Or lying,' said Manolis. 'He's a communist after all.'

'I'm not a communist,' said George.

'You sound like one to me,' said Manolis.

'You don't have to be a communist to ask why someone isn't paid his wages!'

'It's none of your business!'

'This is a distraction,' said the Colonel. 'We're not getting any closer to the truth.'

'I hope you're satisfied, Colonel?' said Yerakas.

Sotiriou gave him a heavy look. 'Nothing I have heard has satisfied me. Your son, your supervisor and his men will have to make sworn statements to the police. When those have been carefully examined I shall let you know if I am satisfied.'

'If we can help any further...'

'I'll let you know.'

Yerakas stood up. 'Let me show you out.'

The 'team' stood aside as George, Colonel Sotiriou and Haris followed Yerakas out of the door into a short passage leading to the hall. George heard Haris say something which he did not catch. Suddenly a scuffle broke out. He turned and saw one of the supervisor's men grab Haris by the lapels of his jacket. Manolis raised a truncheon above Haris' head.

'Watch out!' cried George, but his friend was already butting his head into the face of the man holding him. There was a nasty crack, he twisted away and drove a punch into the stomach of Manolis who was standing poised to strike. The truncheon fell to the floor as Manolis staggered forward.

'Stop this!' barked Yerakas.

'Let me hit the bastard,' said Manolis, reaching for his truncheon.

'No!' said Yerakas.

'He insulted you, Mr Simeon.'

'Forget it.'

Manolis glanced at one of his men, who tried to jump Haris from behind. Haris, sensing the danger, turned to face him, flicked a left jab into the man's face and a swift-footed kick into his crotch. The man toppled away. At once two more lunged forward, but Yerakas stepped in.

'That's enough!' he shouted. 'Anyone who moves loses his

job! That includes you, Manolis! My guests are leaving, and you are going to let them leave in peace.'

He turned to Haris. 'You're lucky I didn't hear what you said, Mr Pezas. If I had, I would have let them destroy you.'

Haris said nothing, but his eyes were filled with fury.

Shepherded by Yerakas, who stood between them and his men, the Colonel, George and Haris walked down the steps to the grey Citroën, where the driver was waiting.

Yerakas watched coolly as they got into the car.

'Mihali,' he said 'will you please take care of the gate?'

As they climbed into the car, Haris muttered, 'Be ready for anything. This isn't over yet.'

The driver started the engine and, watched by Yerakas and his son, set off down the drive. The 'team' had disappeared.

'You showed Manolis a thing or two,' said George.

'He's a bloody psycho. I won't be happy till we're out of here.'

'Don't worry,' said the Colonel. 'It's over.'

'I doubt it,' said Haris.

'What did you say to him?' asked George.

'Something unflattering about his manhood.'

'Why?'

'To test him. I told you, the guy's a psycho. Paranoid and completely out of control. He's your man, Colonel!'

'I'll have him in for questioning, with the rest of his squad. That bandaged hand may well have a story to tell.'

They reached the gate and waited for it to open.

George said, 'Let me call. They've forgotten.'

'The hell they've forgotten. We should get out of the car.'

'What?'

290

'Out, quickly!'

'What's going on?' asked the Colonel.

'Just get out of the fucking car!'

Haris opened his door and pulled George out after him. 'Over there,' he pointed to a clump of bushes by the side of the road. 'Come on, Colonel, out! You're in a death trap.'

Ruled by the urgency in his voice, the Colonel and the driver pushed open their doors and scuttled out.

'Over here,' said Haris. 'Now!'

The Colonel strolled over and said, 'Mr Pezas, you're being melodramatic. Why don't…'

'Keep quiet!' said Haris.

'What are we waiting for?'

A sudden rush of air around them provided the answer. The rear window of the car was smashed in with a loud bang and a cloud of smoke and flame exploded from inside. A second explosion followed, then a third. Fire engulfed the car.

'Dear God,' breathed the Colonel. 'What was that?'

'M32,' said Haris. 'Six-shot grenade pistol. I knew they'd pull some shit like that.' He glanced around. 'Wait for the word, then we'll run. Round the side of the car so we're not seen against the flames. Ready? Follow me.'

Keeping low, they ran down to the fence, then left, towards the heat of the blazing car. Haris held up his hand. He turned to the others. 'When I drop my hand we go, and fast. If they see us, we've had it. We'll let the fire die down: less heat, less light. Then we go at my signal. Wait for it.'

The flames raged on as they watched. George crouched, ready to run. Haris' hand moved slightly, as if about to drop, then stopped. They could hear voices and the tramp of boots approaching.

'Damn!' said Haris under his breath.

He pointed over his shoulder. They crept back towards the shelter of the bushes. Against the fading flames of the car they could see five men. They were joking as they approached.

'How do you like your police, Manolis? Rare or well done?'

'Well done. With barbecue sauce.'

'These ones may be a little burnt.'

'That's fine. Nice and crisp.'

'They'll just be bones now.'

'The dogs can eat them.'

Then one, less jokey. 'You sure they're in there?'

'Of course they're in there!'

'I don't see anyone.'

'Maybe they just vaporised?'

'That doesn't happen.'

'You get a skeleton.'

'So where are they?'

'They don't just burn up.'

'They couldn't have got out.'

'How could they?'

'Look! The car's empty!'

As the realisation dawned, the five men became tense, alert, reaching hurriedly for their weapons. George glanced at Haris, who had a pistol in his hand and was looking at the Colonel. The Colonel nodded grimly. Haris nodded to George, who drew the Beretta from its holster and slipped the safety catch. They both took careful aim. In the corner of his eye George saw the driver do the same. One man each, that would be three shots. They would have to be on target. That would leave two, who would have time to shoot back. Risky, but what could they do? There was another risk too, thought George. This was an execution. Legally questionable, and the Colonel must know it. The correct thing…

Suddenly, the Colonel's voice rang out: 'Drop your weapons and put your hands up. This is a police order.'

The men looked to Manolis. He stood still, saying nothing, eyes glancing nervously about. Slowly he raised one hand, an ambiguous gesture that was neither surrender nor defiance.

'What the hell's that supposed to mean?' muttered Haris.

'Drop your weapons,' said the Colonel again.

Mistake, thought George. That would give them a direction. An instant later, the men opened fire, bullets crackling out of a jagged blaze of orange flame. Haris fired back. One of the men dropped, the others ducking as they continued to shoot. George fired at a crouching dark shape, a much smaller target. Shots jabbered from the bushes, a returning flash burst from the darkness low down in front of them, and someone groaned. George aimed at the flash and fired twice more, and there was silence.

They waited. No sound, no movement; the night closing in round the shrinking ball of firelight.

'I've been hit,' said the driver.

'Badly?'

'I don't know. It's my arm.'

'Let's get out,' said Haris, 'while we can.'

They ran down the hill towards Nea Makri, their footsteps loud in the darkness, the scent of pine trees and the cold air sharp in their nostrils. No one spoke. George tried to calm his racing thoughts.

Colonel Sotiriou was the first to speak. 'I'm going to call for assistance,' he said, 'but first I want to be clear about what we say. There are five dead men back there. Questions will be asked. Our stories must tally.'

'It was self-defence,' said Haris.

'When you're asked to give a statement, say exactly what you saw, exactly what happened. Understood?'

'Including your consent to shoot?'

The Colonel hesitated a moment. 'That too,' he said at last.

He took his phone from his pocket and had a short conversation.

'We'll be picked up at the bottom,' he said. 'Where the main road passes across. Don't worry, Dino. We'll get a doctor to look at your arm. Let's keep going. It's cold.'

39

George let himself and Haris into his flat just after midnight. The sitting room and kitchen were dark, a bar of dim light showing under the door of the spare bedroom.

'I could do with a whisky,' said George. 'How about you?'

Haris nodded.

In the sitting room George switched on a desk lamp. They each took an armchair and stared into the pool of light. The scotch burned in their throats, its warmth a comfort in the desolate cold and blankness of the hour. They had killed. Almost been killed themselves. It was not a good feeling.

After several minutes of silence, George asked, 'How did you know the car was going to be attacked?'

'I knew they would try something. I told you, Manolis is a psycho. Correction: *was.*'

'The Colonel couldn't believe it.'

'At least they won't have to bother with a trial. He's used that cudgel for the last time.'

George shuddered.

Haris went on. 'Yerakas will be devastated.'

'Why? Manolis was just a thug.'

'Not Manolis! His son.'

'What about him?'

'Didn't you see him?'

'Where?'

'By the car. He was one of the five.'

'Are you sure?'

'I saw him.'

'Jesus. That's terrible.'

'He was a fool to go with them.'

George tried to absorb this, thinking of Nick. Yerakas would indeed be devastated. Yet every one of those men, fool or not, was somebody's son.

A sound came from the darkness. A door-handle turning. For a moment George was alarmed. Then a figure materialised, in a dressing gown, with bare feet and loose hair.

'Margaret?'

'Hello,' she said dozily.

'Did we wake you?'

'I was only half asleep,' she said. 'Waiting for you to get back. Hello, Haris!'

'Do you want a drink?' said George.

'No. I just came out to see who it was.'

'Are the children all right?' asked Haris.

'They're fine.' She smiled sleepily. 'I'm so grateful to you both.'

'Happy to help,' said George.

'You two look totally shattered. Are you OK?'

'Yeah, we're fine.'

'Really?'

'Just had a tough night's work.'

'Sleep well then.'

She turned and walked softly back into the bedroom.

'We'd better have another scotch,' said George.

He poured a second shot into each glass, marvelling at the strange power of this fluid, its smoky scent, its golden tint in the lamplight, its oily traces as it splashed and settled.

They continued talking, sometimes lapsing into silence, reflecting on all that happened and was likely to happen now.

'Yerakas won't let this pass,' said George. 'He's a vengeful type, doesn't like to lose. Even a game of tennis. Imagine… his son!'

'He'll be up against the Colonel.'

'That won't stop him.'

'Sotiriou's totally determined. And fearless.'

'He'll have to be.'

They agreed that their part of the job was done. There could be an investigation following those deaths in the hills above Marathon, or there could not. Things would unfold in the inevitably slow, laborious, Byzantine way, and then be forgotten in the maelstrom of further events. Whichever way, they had the argument of self-defence on their side, and evidence to support it.

'Has justice been done?' asked George.

'Can it ever be done?' asked Haris. 'I mean truly done?'

There was no one to answer them. And so they drank to being alive, to surviving in spite of it all – the crisis, the corruption, the endless impunity – and sat on in the half-darkness, saying nothing, thinking overtime, till sleep at last came over them.

Recommended Reading

If you have enjoyed reading *Dangerous Days* there are two more George Zafiris novels to read: *Codename Xenophon* and *Blood & Gold*.

We have also published several other crime novels which explore the society in which they are based and offer a quirky and original read which you might like to try:

Dragon's Eye – Andy Oakes
Citizen One – Andy Oakes
Mensah – Gbontwi Anyetei
Gabriel's Bureau – Mikka Haugaard
The Dream Maker – Mikka Haugaard

We have published four novels by the Greek author Yoryis Yatromanolakis:

The History of a Vendetta
A Report of a Murder
Eroticon
The Spiritual Meadow

And one anthology of Greek writing:

The Dedalus Book of Greek Fantasy – edited by David Connolly

These books can be bought from your local bookshop or online from amazon.co.uk or direct from Dedalus, either online or by post. Please write to **Cash Sales, Dedalus Limited, 24-26, St Judith's Lane, Sawtry, Cambs, PE28 5XE.**

For further details of the Dedalus list please go to our website: www.dedalusbooks.com or write to us for a catalogue.